together

Other Books by Tom Sullivan

Fiction

Alive Day

Nonfiction

If You Could See What I Hear

You Are Special

The Leading Lady (with Betty White)

Special Parent, Special Child

Seeing Lessons: 14 Lessons I've Learned Along the Way

Adventures in Darkness

Children's Books

Common Senses

That Nelson

Adventures in Darkness, children's version

together

A Novel of Shared Vision

Tom Sullivan
with Betty White

THOMAS NELSON
Since 1798

NASHVILLE DALLAS MEXICO CITY RIO DE JANEIRO BEIJING

To all the dogs who make it possible for disabled people to become abled through their love, intelligence, and unwaivering commitment.

Published in Nashville, Tennessee, by Thomas Nelson. Thomas Nelson is a registered trademark of Thomas Nelson, Inc.

Thomas Nelson books may be purchased in bulk for educational, business, fund-raising, or sales promotional use. For information, please e-mail SpecialMarkets@ThomasNelson.com.

Publisher's Note: This novel is a work of fiction. Names, characters, places, and incidents are either products of the author's imagination or used fictitiously. All characters are fictional, and any similarity to people living or dead is purely coincidental.

ISBN 978-1-59554-575-6 (TP)

Library of Congress Cataloging-in-Publication Data

Sullivan, Tom, 1947–
Together : a story of shared vision / Tom Sullivan, with Betty White.
p. cm.
ISBN 978-1-59554-456-8
1. Human-animal relationships—Fiction. 2. Blind—Fiction. 3. Life change events—Fiction. 4. Dogs—Fiction. 5. Mountaineers—Fiction. I. White, Betty, 1922– II. Title.
PS3569.U35925T64 2008
813'.54—dc22 2008009937

Printed in the United States of America

09 10 11 12 RRD 6 5 4 3 2 1

chapter one

It was noon—when the sun was at its highest point and the dog was at his lowest moments. There was an aching in the black Labrador retriever's heart as he circled the area where his people had left him. If he could, he would be asking the question why. *Why did you drive into this park, open the door, bring me out, hug me, pat me, and then leave me?* But dogs never ask questions like that, and they never question if they should love us forever, because love is an absolute. And they don't operate in real time, so for the big animal, returning to the spot where he had been left was something he did as part of his daily routine. And since the ache in his heart wouldn't go away, he would continue to return to that very spot, with the sun sitting high in the sky, and walk in a circle, with his nose down to the ground, hoping to pick up the scent of the humans he loved.

Actually, the young Lab had never met a human being he

didn't like, and as he adapted to his surroundings in San Francisco's Golden Gate Park, he naturally began to befriend everyone with whom he came in contact, with the exception of the ducks who inhabited Stow Lake. These quacking creatures just didn't understand the game. He was supposed to chase them, on land or swimming in the water, wasn't he? That quacking sound they made—it was wonderful. He loved it when they flapped their wings and flew out of the way of his charging enthusiasm. Because, naturally, they were supposed to run away. That was how the game was played, but a few of them just wouldn't budge. And a couple of them even chased him, hissing and drooling as they scooted after him. Still, he could play this game for hours until he was completely exhausted, lying on the grass with his tongue hanging out, panting hard in blissful doggy contentment.

At the far end of the park, he found another activity he couldn't resist. In warmer weather, humans hit little hard balls with a stick, and as soon as the ball was struck, he would run after it, pick it up, and bring it back. Off he would gallop with the humans yelling, "No, dog, no. Leave it alone. Leave the golf ball alone." Okay, okay, he got it. He understood. He didn't have to pick the thing up. The fun was in chasing it. Occasionally, he'd come across a human who would appreciate it when he brought the ball back, so he would follow that person for a while and wait politely for another ball to be hit. After the game he would wander over to where the people were eating food, and often if he wagged his tail enough, one of them would share a delicious hamburger.

He drank from the lake whenever he was thirsty, and he'd found another ready source of food just outside the San Francisco

Botanical Gardens. The big dog had wagged his way into the heart of a street vendor selling hot dogs, and this very good man usually saved six or seven especially for the dog's arrival just after the lunch crowed.

It was at the National AIDS Memorial Grove that he met the human who slept outside like him. This man would cuddle with the big dog on cold nights, and his hugs reminded the animal of how very good it had felt when he was just a few weeks old and slept snuggled against his brothers and sisters.

During the day, the man would stand at an entrance to the park and make a very pleasant sound with his voice and something that he held in his hands. The dog really liked the . . . what was the word he had heard? . . . *music*. It made him feel happy, but at noon he knew it was time to go back to the place where he had been left. Maybe his people would be there. His animal clock would always tell him he needed to be waiting in just the right spot with the sun straight up in the sky, and he would hope—a constant feeling in his doggy heart.

ENRIQUE RAMIREZ WAS TROUBLED by his job. Growing up in Chihuahua, Mexico, on a farm and working the fields, there had always been lots of dogs around, and from the time he was a little boy he had always loved them. His mother used to say that Enrique could never pass up helping a lost stray dog, and so their small house was always full of animals that the family couldn't afford to feed or take care of.

Enrique didn't know why he loved dogs so much, but he

thought it was because of their honesty—and the fact that, in his mind, all they wanted was to be loved by people, and that seemed to him to be the right way to live. Working for the SPCA over the last five years, he had never, ever been bitten by an animal. In fact, he couldn't even remember when any of the dogs he had picked up had growled at him or been really upset when he enticed them into his van.

He knew he had a way with animals, and he was sure that they knew he cared about them. He tried not to think about the dogs he brought in when he considered that many of them would never find good homes and would have to be—what was that gringo word they used?—yes, euthanized. That seemed to be a big word for something he believed to be cruel and unnecessary. So, sometimes he asked himself why he did the job, and his answer was always the same. The animals he took off the street could never make it on their own. The best chance they had, he knew, was that the SPCA would find people to love them, so he continued to try and do his job in the best way possible.

Right now he was studying a young black Lab—probably not even one year old—that seemed to have a very specific purpose. He watched as the dog circled in a small area with his nose down to the ground, as if he must be looking for something. Enrique had seen this behavior before, and he knew that this animal was one of those who must have been abandoned and was now waiting for his master to return. *How could people do that*, he thought, *just leave these beautiful creatures to suffer or even starve?*

"All right," he told himself, "that's why I do this job. I can save some of them, and that is the right thing to do."

Climbing out of his truck and taking a couple of doggy treats from his pocket, he moved slowly in the direction of the dog and began to gain the animal's attention by talking softly and shaking the treats in his hand. The dog's head came up from what he had been doing, and Enrique believed he could almost see the animal smile with pleasure.

This is one of the ones who really likes people, he thought. *This one won't be hard at all.*

"Come on, boy," he said persuasively. "Come on over and have a treat."

The handsome dog trotted over and took a biscuit from the man's hand as if he had known him forever.

"That's a good boy," the man said soothingly, and the sound of his voice made the Lab wag his tail. "That's a good boy," he said again. "Now just stand still and let me put a leash on you."

Enrique took a heavy nylon lead from his pocket, and the Lab didn't object at all as the lead went over his neck.

Very good, the man thought. *Very good.*

"Come on, boy," he said. "Come on. Come with me."

Enrique took two steps, and in that moment the big dog understood that the man wanted to move him away from his place, away from his mission to wait for his masters to come back.

No, the Lab registered. *No!* And he dug all four feet into the ground, whining as if he was hurt.

"It's all right," the man said. "It's okay, boy. I'm not going to hurt you. Come on, boy, let's go. Come on now, boy."

The animal was even more determined not to leave his place,

not to give up. He pulled hard in the other direction, tightening the sliding lead around his neck, nearly choking himself with the effort.

The man was quick to respond. Stepping forward he snapped a muzzle around the black Lab's nose and placed his hands under the dog's chest, lifting him into the air, making him helpless.

Now the big animal found himself tossed into the back of the van, unhurt but visibly upset. Everything in his doggy head was crying, *No, no! My people will be back. I know they'll come back. I can't leave this place. I can't ever leave this place.*

Enrique looped the handle of the leash around a tie-down and closed the van doors.

"I'm sorry, boy," he said. "I'm very sorry. I hope you find a good home. I really hope you'll find a home."

THIRTY MINUTES LATER, THE YOUNG Lab was being registered and going through the intake process of vet checks and shots. The muzzle had been removed because the animal clearly wasn't interested in biting anyone or hurting the people. All that he was feeling was a deep, deep sadness because now there would be no master coming to get him. He was not in the right place. He was not where he should be.

He was in a four-by-eight-foot area surrounded by concrete, except for the wire mesh fencing that allowed him to look out and people to look in. He was given water and food by some humans who spoke in very soft, soothing tones, but it was hard to hear them over the noise of all the other dogs. None of the animals were happy, including the big Lab, and no one slept very much, as day and night didn't matter at all because there wasn't any sun.

Sometimes new people came and spoke to the dogs, and sometimes dogs were taken out of the cages and not brought back. People spoke to him too, but they were not his people. Even though he had been taken from his place, he knew his people would come—he just knew they would come.

HE WATCHED THE MAN AND the excited little boy move down the line of cages and dogs. He watched because something about the man said *kind*—said *good*. He watched as they talked to other dogs up and down the line, and he waited for them to come and see him.

"What about this one, Uncle Smitty?" the boy was saying as he pointed to a dog next to him. "I like this one."

"Well, Danny, you might have picked just the perfect one," the man said. "She looks like a combination of spaniel and . . . let's see . . . maybe . . . hm. There might be border collie in her. That would be an interesting combination because she would be playful with you. In fact," the man laughed, "she'd probably chase you around, biting your feet, herding you like you were a sheep. That's what border collies do. And she'd have that spaniel kind of quality; just the perfect dog to cuddle at night. Let's see if we can take her out of the cage and go into a room where we can sit on the floor and socialize with her."

While the man was speaking, his practiced eye was watching

the black Lab. The young animal's eyes showed intelligence, and the man instictively moved to the big animal's cage, placing his palms against the wire and dropping down on his knees to the level of the dog.

"Hello, boy," he said. "Why are you in here?"

The dog liked the sound of the man, so he stood up, placing his nose against the wire and wagging his tail. The man put his face against the cage from the other side and blew gently into the Lab's nose—a sign of love and connection going back to the wolf. The dog responded, trying to lick the man but only rubbing his tongue on the wire.

"Good boy," the man said. "You really are a good boy, and you're handsome. Gosh, you're handsome. You're a perfect-looking black Lab. Somebody really made a mistake abandoning you. I'll bet you even have papers. You certainly come from good breeding. You know what? Let me help Danny find a new friend, and I'll be back to see you, okay?"

The man turned back to his nephew, and involuntarily—for the first time since he had been in captivity—the dog whined.

The man laughed. "Okay, pal, okay," he said. "I told you I'll be back, and I will."

Over the next half hour, the man helped the boy socialize with his new friend, and it could not have gone better. The little border collie/spaniel mix loved to play and cuddle, and the boy could not have been happier.

"What are you going to name her?"

"I don't know, Uncle Smitty," the boy said furrowing his brow, "but I think I might name her Abigail."

"Abigail?" the man said, surprised at the choice. "Why Abigail?"

"Well, my sister has a doll named Abigail, and I like the name."

"That's good," Uncle Smitty said. "You could call her Abby for short."

"What do you think of that, Abby?" the boy asked. "Is Abby or Abigail okay with you?"

On cue, the little dog licked his face, drawing a peal of happy laughter.

"All right, then," the man said, "Abigail it is. Now, Danny, you stay here with Abigail for a few minutes. I just want to take another look at the dog that was living next to her, okay?"

The man borrowed a leash from one of the SPCA volunteers and got permission to take the young Lab out into the parking lot. The animal was surprised, but the man's voice and the way he touched him and scratched his ears just so made him happy enough to keep wagging his tail.

"I don't know if you've had any training," the man said. "You're pretty young, but let's fool around a little, okay?"

The man began to teach the animal to heel and sit, and the big dog loved it. When he got the idea what the man wanted, it was natural for him to want to please, and the man saw it immediately.

"You know what? You might just be one of the good ones; one of the very, very good ones. And I might just have the job that will make your life special. What do you think of that, boy?"

The dog looked up at the man as if to say, *I think that would be fine, just fine.*

A half hour later, the man's car pulled out of the SPCA parking lot with the man and the boy in front and two very happy dogs sharing the backseat.

chapter two

The young man stood, silhouetted against what he believed to be the bluest sky on earth. As always, he felt at one with the mountain, never conquering it, only sharing its beauty with all of nature's creations lucky enough to ascend its peak. For a brief second, he shivered as the whitest of white clouds passed overhead, temporarily blocking the intense noonday sun. It was the summer solstice, June 21, when the great orb stood above the equator and time was suspended as the earth balanced precariously on the edge of the changing seasons.

Today, Brenden McCarthy was in the Elk Range above Aspen, Colorado, at the top of the Maroon Bells. In actual fact, his feet were planted firmly on North Maroon, the toughest of the Bells to climb. It was a moment of utter happiness.

In McCarthy's short life—twenty-five years and six months, to be exact—he had climbed all fifty-four peaks of fourteen thousand feet and above in the state of Colorado. Climbing was his passion—or rather, one of them. He was just as passionate about becoming a great orthopedic surgeon.

Having just graduated from the University of Colorado medical school, he was in his first year of residency at St. Joseph Hospital, overwhelmed by work but somehow loving the experience.

That's who Brenden McCarthy was—a young man who loved the experience of being alive. This morning he drove up from Denver on his prized possession—a rebuilt 1959 Harley Panhead motorcycle that took every penny he could scrounge from jobs he worked all through undergraduate school at Colorado State. The bike was a total trip as it roared along I-70 traveling west and turned onto Route 82, crossing Castle Creek and then turning south on an access road that allowed him to be more aggressive. He pulled in and wheelied to a stop in the parking lot of Maroon Lake Campground.

He knew he was showing off, but on this Thursday there wasn't anyone around. And frankly, he just couldn't help himself. With this perfect weather, he figured the climb would take around six and a half hours with the descent actually slower than the ascent because of having to be so careful of a mountain climber's most deadly enemy—scree—loose rock that at any time could send even the most experienced climber plummeting to—what? Injury? Death? Brenden didn't want to know.

He shook off the thought as he began to prepare for the climb. Today he chose a familiar route to the top of North Maroon. Though he was dressed in shorts, a T-shirt, heavy socks, and hiking boots, he was experienced enough always to be completely prepared. In his daypack he carried a simple but appropriate hiker's first-aid kit—a bottle of water, along with a filtering pump that would allow him to take water from mountain springs, power bars and a banana for energy, and a gigantic tuna fish sandwich. He also never climbed without a signal mirror, compass, and topographical map that he certainly didn't need but was never without. As an Eagle Scout, he never forgot the axiom "Be prepared."

McCarthy was a young man exacting in all things, and it was this quality of exactness that allowed him to seem to others to be a completely free spirit. His father had always said preparation and perspiration allow for expectation and inspiration. McCarthy believed that was true, so additionally, his clothing consisted of a heavy woolen cap that could be pulled down over his ears, a woolen scarf his mother gave him that seemed a little effeminate but that he secretly loved, a long-sleeved shirt that could be covered by a down vest, and a Gore-Tex windproof jacket. He also carried long underwear that could fit under his shorts and heavy Gore-Tex pants with plenty of pocket space. Two pairs of gloves, extra socks, a flashlight, whistle, and ice axe completed his equipment.

As he checked over his stuff one more time, he read the history of these great peaks on a large plaque at the base of the ascent. The Maroon Bells were so named because of their pyramid-like shape and astounding native maroon color that changed to fire red when emblazoned by the sun.

Mountain historians Lampert and Borneman referred to the

Bells as red, rugged, and rotten because of the unpredictability of their sedimentary surfaces. The history went on to say that North Maroon Peak was the fiftieth highest of the fifty-four Colorado peaks, measuring 14,014 feet.

He was surprised to read that the mountains were sometimes called "The Deadly Bells" because more than on any other Colorado peaks, unprepared climbers lost their lives. The complexity of the tree roots and the rock often spelled disaster. In 1965, for example, six climbers ascended the Bells and never came down.

The Haden and Wheeler surveys in the mid-1890s first mapped the Bells, and the first documented ascent had been completed in 1908.

So, here was Brenden, a century later, feeling like the luckiest young guy in the world as he began to climb. The route for his ascent was based around a series of ledges that measured eight to ten feet in height. Brenden always thought of this particular climb as being like ascending the Washington Monument or maybe the Lincoln Memorial. There were literally hundreds of these steps, and he was forced to snake his way up them very much in the way one might ski down one of the sister slopes of Aspen.

As he moved laterally back and forth across the mountain, he kept his eyes down in search of stone cairns—piles of rock left by other climbers indicating the places where he could scramble up to the top of the next ledge.

Brenden's climb began from the campground at 9,600 feet, moving southwest along a well-beaten hiking path and skirting

Maroon Lake. He continued for about a mile and a half before he stopped and caught his breath at the beauty of Crater Lake, a volcanic crater filled with water as pristine as anyone had ever seen.

Then came a half-mile climb up the steep Minnehaha Trail that forced even this very physically fit young man to take deep breaths as he exerted his will on the mountain. Arriving at the top of the trail, he looked back and saw the last of the campgrounds at Buckskin Pass.

Then, turning south and fording a small creek, Brenden began the main part of the climb up a prominent gully that reached to what looked to him like a round island of rock surrounded by green, thickly layered mountain meadow grasses. Then it was time to cross the Ancient Glacier, being oh so careful of loose rock, until he reached the northeast face and began ascending a couloir. These couloir, as they were called, were like divots in the mountain, allowing the climber to press himself against the sidewalls as he worked his way up.

Brenden breathed like a bellows when he reached the top of the couloir. But he gathered his strength while crossing a flat ledge that took him to a second couloir and a final ascent to the north base, bringing him to the summit.

So, here he was with his chin tilted up to the warmth of the noonday sun, believing that Robert Burns was right: all has to be in its heaven. All has to be right with the world, or at least that's how God designed it. Brenden was comfortable in the thought that there were screwups in the environment. But these were all on man's shoulders. God had nothing to do with them.

Brenden felt a lump in his throat as his eyes swept over the panorama that surrounded him. The combination of toylike forms and colors as seen from this mountaintop delighted him, giving rise to feelings of joy, appreciation, and sheer awe in the vivid majesty before him.

He was two thousand feet above timberline, and the scrubbed pine below looked like miniature Christmas trees decorated with the sunlit yellow-gold of thousands of aspens reaching hungrily skyward.

Brenden reluctantly remembered that he had not yet honored the climber's tradition. Moving a few feet to his left, he reached the summit block, a stick in the ground with a two-foot-long piece of PVC pipe wedged tightly between two rocks at its base. Unscrewing one of the ends, he removed a folded parchment, a document on which all climbers logged their dates and times of arrival.

These scrolls were kept by the Colorado Mountain Club and published in various climbing publications. Climbers didn't sign for glory. They respectfully stated their achievement of the summit with gratitude to the mountain for allowing them to succeed.

He sat down on a rock outcropping and began to wolf down his lunch.

Boy, am I hungry, he thought. *I missed breakfast, and this tastes delicious. Something about altitude air, I guess.*

In the distance he noticed the white contrails of a jet leaving the Aspen airport as it cut its way through the crystal blue sky. Between bites, he let his eyes wander back to the valley below.

He noted the minimansions across from downtown Aspen looking like dollhouses built by the hands of miniarchitects. *There is civilization*, he thought, *interacting fairly well with the natural order of things in these mountains*.

Still looking east but above and beyond the town, he could see Mount Massive and Mount Albert, the highest of the Colorado fourteeners. Turning slightly to the north and shading his eyes, he could make out the outline of Mount Holy Cross, though the cross itself was hidden from view on the east face. A little more to the northwest, he traced the slender outline of Snowmass and Maroon Peak, the second and third of the Bells.

He brought his eyes back south and took in the vista of Pyramid Peak, looming so close he felt he could almost touch it. This was a mountain he loved to climb. Beyond he could also see Castle Peak. And because the day was so clear, in the far distance he could make out the outlines of the mountains that made up the San Juan Range.

Never, he realized, would he ever take any of this for granted. He was at the top of the world, relishing one of the best moments of his life.

And now he wasn't alone. He heard her cry before he saw her: a golden eagle, diving for a pika and getting it. There was now one less rodent on the mountain and an eagle to share lunch with. He watched as the bird chewed its prey, sitting motionless on the thermals.

Now there's something I wish I could do, he thought, *sit up there all day and not have to work hard.* "You're beautiful," he called to the eagle. "Beautiful."

The bird moved her wings slightly, like a princess acknowledging the presence of a commoner.

Okay, bird, he thought. *I get it. It's your sky, but today it's my mountain.*

By the angle of the sun he reckoned it to be just after two o'clock. Time to start down, he knew. Even though the light would last until well after 8 p.m., he never wanted to run the risk of not getting down before dark, especially when all he had with him was a daypack.

He allowed himself a fifteen-minute nap, resting on the warmth of the sunny rock with his jacket as a pillow. Call it a catnap or dognap or people-nap, when he stood and stretched, he felt amazing—at one with his own physicality, at peace with his emotional state, connected to the earth, and ready to return to civilization and all the challenges that were waiting for him.

He began working his way back down the exact route he had ascended. He was careful but catlike as he moved over the loose scree. Though it sometimes moved under his foot, he was on to the next stone before danger could threaten. His eyes never stopped evaluating the placement of his feet, and he had an uncanny sense, developed over years of climbing, regarding the feel of the rock. He was like a ballet dancer with a wirewalker's appreciation for the risks involved.

He had been descending for about an hour and a half when he came to a particularly squirrelly area of loose junk—he never used the word *scree*—made worse by the runoff from a mountain stream.

Careful now, he reminded himself. *Be very careful. Don't rush.*

A whir just to the right and above him made him turn his head, and from the corner of his eye he once again saw the beautiful eagle diving for something to eat. Later he would wonder if the turning of his head changed the angle of his foot plant or broke his concentration. All he knew for sure was that the fall began oh so slowly.

Rock slid from under his boots. Slow falls are the ones that kill you, mountaineers say, because you work so hard to maintain balance that you lose it.

Like the wirewalker knowing in an instant that there's no net below, Brenden understood this. He had time to think about it as he desperately competed with gravity to maintain his balance.

For a moment he thought he'd make it as he sort of slalomed along the top of the sliding stone. But then he tipped forward, his chin dropping to his chest—a human bowling ball bouncing down a natural alley to strike stone pins that could not be knocked down.

He screamed, or he thought he screamed, as he bounced along. He heard more than felt the crack of his climbing helmet as his head tattooed the boulders. All of this might have taken mere seconds—almost no time at all in the scheme of life—but the impact would resound forever in the man he would become.

Unconscious now, he continued to careen along until finally he came to a blessed stop against an outcropping that probably saved his life.

The mountains give, and the mountains take. How Brenden would come to understand that fundamental truth.

chapter three

Bart knew he was in trouble. The big, black Labrador lay with his head on his paws, listening to Lady as she screamed at him. When she yelled this loud, he knew she was really mad. The dog raised his head and sat up when Lady waved the shoe she had just taken from him—or at least what was left of it. The high heel that had come off was still in his mouth.

"Look what you've done! My new shoes! You are a bad, bad dog! BAD! I can't take this anymore!"

Hearing the commotion, the dog's master came in to investigate. Being blind, he couldn't see the damage, but his wife's fury made the situation clear.

Man didn't yell, but Bart could tell from his voice that he wasn't happy.

"Calm down, honey. How did he get hold of them? Did you leave them on the floor?"

"Don't you dare try and blame me for this. I told you the last time this happened that I have had all I can take. What do I mean, the last time—there've been too many times. I'm through with this animal!"

"You don't mean that, dear. You know how much I need him. He helps me more than—"

Lady cut him off. "Oh sure, *you're* fine. Strolling around the neighborhood or showing off to your friends. What about me? What about the turkey? What about the Christmas tree? When he knocked it over, who had to clean up the mess? Not you! Sometimes I get the feeling that dog's more important to you than I am." She paused for breath, but not for long. "Make up your mind; either he goes or I do!"

Slamming the broken shoe into the wastebasket, she stormed out of the room, the man right behind her.

The big, black dog was always tense when he heard them argue, but this time seemed worse than usual. He lost all interest in the shoe heel and for once didn't automatically follow the man but slid to the floor and stayed where he was, his chin between his paws. He could hear their voices, still raised, going on and on in the other room.

Bart liked Man, but he didn't understand Lady.

Why did she talk so loud?

A picture came into the dog's mind.

The loudest he had ever heard her yell was that day with the turkey. Oh, it smelled so good when they were eating it. Afterward, she put it up on top of the fridge. If he wasn't supposed to touch it, then why did she put it where he could reach it? All he had to do was put his paws up on the door and pull it down. She must have heard the platter break—she sure came running. But he got some of it. Oh, he was sick after. *Real* sick. Man tried to help, but Lady acted mad at both of them. She really yelled that time.

Soon the angry voices calmed somewhat and eventually ceased altogether. The dog stood up and shook himself hard enough to rattle his collar. He hoped things were good again.

Time to go check on dinner.

"YES. IT *IS* TOO BAD. I'm very sorry to hear it. So—I'll make the arrangements and get back to you. No, I understand. Thank you."

Hanging up, Smitty sat very still, his frown deepening, his hand still on the phone.

Beth turned from the file cabinet. She had been Smitty's assistant for too long not to recognize an unusual reaction for this normally upbeat man.

"Problem?" she asked.

Smitty's tight voice reflected his frustration.

"It's Bart again. The partnership didn't work out. He's being returned." Smitty sighed. "I really thought I'd found the right guy for him, but he's caused so much trouble around the house they're giving up on him and sending him back. What a shame. They did so great in training together."

"Can't you just send somebody to check out the situation?"

Beth knew the protocol. Now and then a dog and the new

blind owner had trouble adjusting when they went home together after the supportive environment of Guide Dog School. It was nothing new. Sometimes it took a couple of follow-up visits from the school personnel to smooth out the rough edges.

Smitty shook his head.

"We've done that twice already."

"Twice?!"

"Twice. Bart's a handful—I admit it. He's such a magnificent guide—one of the best ever—but he's on energy overload. Too much, it seems, to work with a guy who tunes pianos for a living but then just goes home and stays put. Bart loves to work—*loves* it. That's why they did so well in class. I know I broke every rule to get him in guide dog school, talking the bosses into taking this pound puppy. But there's something special about this one—he's going to be an amazing partner for someone. I just know it. When he's in harness, he's perfect—it's his off time when he screws up."

Tossing his glasses on the desk, Smitty pushed his chair back. "I should have seen this coming. I was just hoping . . ." His voice trailed off.

Beth smiled. "Well, you'll just have to find somebody else for—what's his name?—Bart. Maybe he just needs a little more training. He can go into reissue."

Smitty took a long beat. "He's been there."

"What do you mean?"

"This dog's on his third go-around."

"What are you talking about?"

"When he came back the second time, I couldn't bring myself

to put him into career change. He's just too good. You don't know this dog."

Smitty got up and walked to the window. Looking out over the lush green campus he could see a handler exercising a yellow Labrador retriever down below. Farther on, two girls were chatting as they walked a German shepherd and another yellow Lab.

"I changed his name to Bart," he said quietly. "I did some creative record changing and sent him through the program all over again. He knew the stuff already—he must have been bored stiff."

Beth was shocked.

"But that's against all the rules! You'd fire somebody for doing that!"

Smitty had no answer. He just shook his head again.

Beth couldn't let it go.

"Smitty, you've trained more dogs than I can count. They don't all make it—of course not. How come you're so upset about this one?"

Smitty shrugged and went back to his chair.

"I know I'm over the top with this dog, but there is something about him—it's hard to explain. There are a lot of good ones, but the really great ones don't come around that often. I could sense it in him back when I saw him in the pound. I just have a gut feeling that with the right person—a *strong* one—this dog would knock your socks off."

"Sounds like that's what he's been doing already." Beth still didn't get it. "How come somebody didn't recognize him?"

"He only trained with me. Nobody else was that close to

him and"—Smitty allowed himself a small chuckle—"unless you really know them, black Labradors do have a tendency to look a lot like other black Labradors. Nobody picked up on it."

The room was quiet. Beth waited for him to go on. When he didn't, she asked, "So what are you going to do this time?"

"I . . . don't know."

BART MANAGED TO AVOID CONFLICT with Lady by staying out of her way, and a few days passed without incident. Everything seemed back to normal.

This morning started off the same as all the others, with an early walk. Man buckled Bart into his harness, and they headed out into the clear morning air, the energetic dog making sure to put just enough pressure on the harness to lead his blind master.

The quiet neighborhood of tree-lined streets and tended gardens could seem, to anyone who noticed such things, as if the calendar stopped fifty years ago. The other dogs, the children playing, an occasional passerby, even the cats that darted across their path—Bart ignored them all. He was in harness. This was work time.

His regular routine included heading for the little mom-and-pop grocery a few blocks away, where Bart accepted his usual warm greetings while Man bought his sweet rolls and orange juice. Then they headed home. Same as always.

When they got back, Man removed Bart's working harness, then sat down to eat his breakfast with the dog beside him, staring, hoping for a handout.

When the doorbell rang, Man went to answer, Bart at his side. It was no one Bart recognized, but the person was invited in, so the dog greeted him politely, then went over to plop down out of the way. Man called Lady, and the three people sat down to talk.

To Bart, lying on the cool hardwood floor between the rugs—chin on his paws, ears alert—the talk seemed to go on a long time. Now and then they would look over his way, and it didn't take much to know they were talking about him. He didn't raise his head, but his eyebrows twitched as he moved his eyes from one face to the other. Everybody was so serious. They didn't seem happy.

At last they stopped talking, and Man and the person stood up. When Man picked up the harness with the big square handle, Bart got up and moved forward, expecting to be buckled in as usual. He was surprised when Man pushed him away.

"No, Bart. Back."

Instead, Man handed the harness to Person, along with Bart's leash. *His* leash! Then Man bent down and hugged the dog and petted him—hard. The slow wag of tail in response was tentative, questioning, but Man didn't answer.

Lady just sat there.

Person and Man shook hands. They exchanged a few words. Then Person—not Man—clipped the leash to Bart's collar and headed for the door.

Confused, the big dog didn't move.

"Heel, Bart." Person gave the leash a tug. "Come on, boy. Let's go. Bart, heel!"

At the familiar command, Bart reluctantly moved to the door. Person didn't stop but headed on down the front steps toward a car parked at the curb. When they got to the bottom of the stairs, things suddenly felt all wrong to Bart. He pulled back on the leash and turned to see if Man was coming. He was just in time to see the door as it closed.

"Good boy, Bart." Person's voice was warm and reassuring. "It's okay, big guy. Bart, heel!"

But this time the dog would have none of it. He tried to shake loose of the leash, locking all four brakes and desperately pulling back.

Person was patient but firm. Without forcing the issue, he continued to reassure the dog as he worked him step-by-step down the path to the car. Opening the rear car door, he stopped his urging and simply waited. He continued to speak in a warm, low tone, using Bart's name again and again as he rubbed the soft ears and scratched the dog's chest. Bart's rapid heartbeat began to subside.

"Good boy, Bart! In you go."

For this dog, obeying was a way of life, but now it all felt weird. This wasn't the right car. Why wasn't Man coming with them? What was he supposed to do?

Person slowly lifted the dog's front feet up into the car and continued to push until Bart was forced to scramble up onto the backseat.

"Good boy! That's it, Bart—good!"

Closing the door, Person moved around into the driver's seat to start the engine.

The dog sat as if carved in stone—or perhaps ebony. His gaze fixed straight ahead, he didn't even glance out the window as they pulled away from the curb.

This was like another time that he could remember. It was at his other house. He liked those people a lot, until one day somebody came and talked with them. Then Bart was taken away. He never saw those people again.

The pictures in his mind made Bart uncomfortable, prompting a deep and audible sigh. The worst time of all—ever—was the day he lost the special man he loved the most. That was at another place a long time ago. People called that man Smitty, and Bart worked with him every day. Smitty taught him things, and if he did them right, he would get lots of praise—maybe even a treat.

Then one day Smitty took him to that other house with those nice people, but when he went away again, Smitty didn't take Bart with him. He left him there. And he never came back.

Bart finally let his front feet slide until he lay curled up on the car seat, head down, eyes wide open, his mind still full of questions.

Person eventually switched on the radio, and the miles increased. Between the hum of the motor and the motion of the car, the pictures in the dog's mind began to fade and intermingle until he finally fell into a fitful sleep, which lasted until the car turned off the road and stopped beside some gas pumps. Bart sat up and watched as Person got out, put the hose in the tank, and came around to open the door and slide into the seat beside him.

"How you doin', Bart? How about a walk? Bet you might have to go."

Person picked up the leash and got out. "Come on, Bart, let's go *park*."

Bart heard the familiar command and was less resistant this time. He allowed himself to follow the man to a nearby pet area. *Park* meant relieve himself, which he promptly did, then returned to the car without objection.

Back on the road, Bart went to sleep almost immediately, as the best way to pass the time. He didn't know how long they'd been driving when he felt the car turn onto a side road. He stood up but sat again quickly as the curve in the road made balancing difficult. Out the window, he could see the lush, green countryside, and suddenly, for no accountable reason, he felt a small rush of excitement. He didn't notice when Person picked up the cell phone and punched a number, but at Person's first word, the dog froze.

"Smitty? We just turned onto the campus, so we'll be there shortly. Yeah—he's doing okay. It was a little rough at first, but he's doing fine."

The dog was on his feet, curves or not.

"Do you want me to take him to the kennels or bring him to you? No problem—I'll see you in a few minutes. Thanks, Smitty."

There it was again. It had been a long time since Bart heard that word, but there was no mistaking its effect on him. The feeling of excitement increased, and he started to pant.

Buildings began to appear, and the road changed from a highway to a street with a row of low buildings. Bart could see people now and then, some of them accompanied by dogs. He found it all most interesting. He had seen something like this before, and it was becoming more and more familiar. He had been here.

The car turned a corner, then another, and finally pulled to a stop.

Before Person could get out of the car, the glass doors of one of the buildings opened, and a man came out and down the steps toward them.

The dog began to tremble, letting out little choke cries, the black tail beating against the car seat.

Smitty!

Smitty! Smitty! Smitty!

chapterfour

To watch Lindsey Reynolds cross the campus of the University of Denver Sturm College of Law, one would have the immediate impression of a young woman purposeful in every way. And if the camera moved in for a close-up, the impression would go on to say that Lindsey was cocky, bordering on arrogant. The truth was, she knew it, and it was also true that there was good reason for her self-absorbed opinion. Lindsey was great at everything she did and driven to fulfill her personal destiny with unswerving commitment.

As she crossed the campus on that beautiful fall evening, dressed in jeans, flip-flops, and a T-shirt that did not hide the beautiful figure beneath, Lindsey moved with an easy, flowing feminine grace that said she was completely secure in her natural beauty and the effect it had on most people who came in contact with her. Lindsey knew what she wanted and how she planned to get it.

She came to the University of Denver law school after graduating magna cum laude from USC, where she was captain of the volleyball team and senior class president as well as runner-up for homecoming queen—an honor she figured she hadn't won because most of the voters were jealous of her.

Now in her third year, she was sure she'd make law review and join a corporate firm with a starting salary of at least $85K. The cherry had been placed on the cake of her life plan when she met Brenden McCarthy.

Now here is someone ideal, she thought. *He is a laid-back mountain boy who loves the outdoors, but he has the kind of brain that will make him a great surgeon and a terrific husband.*

There was no question in Lindsey's mind that she loved Brenden, but it's hard to love another when you love yourself so much. At the moment she was a wee bit annoyed that she hadn't heard from her mountain-climbing fiancé.

He should have been down a couple of hours ago, and waiting for him had put her behind on her evening's work at the library. It was around eight o'clock, the sun was beginning to set, and she remembered that Brenden always said that climbers should not stay up on a mountain after dark.

She decided to dial his cell phone again. She got his message unit.

"You've reached Brenden. If I don't return your call for a few hours, it's because I'm doing something fun—probably riding a bike or climbing, or, if there's snow on the mountain, skiing. So don't hold it against me if it takes me some time to call you back. Your message is important to me, but so is living."

"Late." Lindsey took a deep breath and waited for the beep. "You know, you've really got to change that message. People could start to think you don't love them. But not me. I know you can't get enough of your lady lawyer. So, when you get this message, call me. I'll be in the library."

IT WAS ON NIGHTS LIKE this that Mora McCarthy missed her husband, Brian, the most. He had been a wonderful partner and a great father. They had both always been so proud of Brenden, but cancer took him before he had the chance to see his son graduate and become a doctor.

They had always been a wonderful family. Brian in the insurance business. Mora substitute teaching, just because she loved it. Brenden, the perfect son. And Bridget, happily married and now living in Washington with their two grandchildren and her political lobbyist husband.

Mora hated setting the table and eating alone on nights like this. She ached with the memories of wonderful conversations she and Brian used to enjoy while they ate a late dinner as the kids did their homework.

Death robs you of so many things, she thought, *but it's the intimacy of love shared with another that is the cruelest part of loss.*

Tonight she left the door to the deck open so that the warm June air could flow through the house. Like her son, she loved natural things. Even in her cooking, she used nothing but fresh ingredients. For this meal, she had prepared handmade linguine with clams in a white sauce, along with a pear salad with Stilton and lightly battered zucchini—all things she knew her son loved.

She was surprised he hadn't arrived for dinner, but she figured maybe he got confused and forgot it was Thursday night.

That's what love will do to you, she reminded herself. *He's head over heels in love with Lindsey. I wish I could slow him down. She's a lot of wonderful things but not necessarily for my son.*

Deciding that she might as well go ahead and eat alone, she sighed and seated herself at the table, feeling sorry enough to remember that her husband was dead, and her son—well, her son just hadn't shown up. She was alone, but not lonely, because Gus sat across from her.

Gus was an extraordinarily brilliant, enthusiastic, loving West Highland terrier who had the capacity to care for the entire family, with a special understanding that made everyone feel that he or she was the most important person in his life. He was Brenden's playmate when the young man was home, creating fun and diversion from the intensity of medical school. He was Mora's constant companion as she did her housework and tended her exceptional garden. And when Brian had become sick, spending most of his time in bed under hospice care, it was Gus who had never left his side.

Mora remembered the dog's black eyes, pleading that his master might get well. She recalled many things about those bad days, but two related specifically to Gus. How the night after the funeral the dog took his position sitting opposite her in Brian's chair, never trying to take any food from the table—just sitting upright, stoic, trying to fill the space for his lonely mistress. And it was Gus who took possession of Brian's favorite sweater, the one he had worn so often while lounging at home on weekends. Mora had let him have it, and Gus never slept without it.

"Okay, Gus, I guess it's just you and me for dinner. Brenden must be having an exceptionally good day."

The telephone jarred her out of her reverie. Picking it up, she looked at the number and realized it wasn't Brenden.

"Hello?"

"Hello, Mrs. McCarthy? It's Spider, I mean, Charlie."

"I know who it is, Charlie." Mora laughed. "If you're looking for Brenden, he's not here."

"Oh, he told me he was having dinner with you tonight."

"He was supposed to. Have you spoken to Lindsey?"

"No, ma'am, but I'll call her. If he comes in, have him give me a call, would you, Mrs. McCarthy? I'd love to borrow his motorcycle tomorrow if I can. I have to be in Aspen for some dry-land training for ski patrol, and it's always fun to borrow Brenden's bike."

"That's where he went, Charlie. I mean, that's where he was today. Climbing the Bells."

There was the slightest pause on the other end of the line.

"And you mean he's not down yet?"

"I don't know. I don't know, Charlie. Should I be worried?" Mora asked, the tension rising slightly in her voice.

"Oh no. Oh no, ma'am," Charlie put in quickly. "He's probably just taking a little longer to get there with traffic and all. I'll call him later. Or have him call me when he comes in, okay?"

"All right, Charlie," Mora said. "I'll have him call."

Putting down the receiver, she felt a chill run down her spine. *Mothers have instincts*, she thought, *and mine are sending me the wrong message.*

Again, she picked up the phone and hit the speed-dial button connecting her to Brenden's cell. Hearing the same message that Lindsey heard earlier, she simply said, "Brenden, it's your mother; call me." That usually was enough to make him respond right away. She hoped so. For some reason, she prayed so.

Charlie "Spider" Evans was also feeling instinctive pangs about his friend, Brenden McCarthy. They had been pals since high school, sharing everything from football to fantasies over cheerleaders. But it was in a mutual love of the outdoors that their friendship had taken on that special intimacy reserved for your lifetime best pal.

Spider knew that Brenden should be off the mountain. He knew it in his gut because he understood how respectful his friend was of the dangers that could confront any climber. And so, Charlie Evans made the call that would send climbers up North Maroon in search of a young man in trouble.

Charlie's first call was to 9-1-1, where he talked to a dispatcher who connected him to the deputy serving as the incident commander. In turn, the commander paged the team leader for Mountain Rescue Aspen, an all-volunteer group of outdoorsmen and women who give their time keeping climbing enthusiasts safe.

Since the rescue group was made up of volunteers, the calls and arrangements to adjust personal schedules took hours. It was four in the morning when fifteen climbers arrived at the staging area cabin on Main Street, Aspen. Charlie also joined them. He was known as a very capable climber and was easily accepted as one of the team searching for Brenden.

Charlie initially believed the fastest way to find his friend would be to do a helicopter drop on the top of the mountain, because he was sure Brenden would have signed the register, indicating his route.

"Sounds good," Commander Jeffries said, "but I've already made a bunch of calls, and we can't get a helicopter up here till around nine thirty or ten o'clock in the morning. By that time, we could already have climbers on the top. It sure would be a lot better if the National Guard birds weren't in Iraq—then we wouldn't have to draw from Denver to get help. So we'll do this the old-fashioned way. The hasty team will push off in about forty-five minutes. Think you can hang with them, Spider?"

Charlie nodded.

"They should be able to get to the top at around eight o'clock. By then, we'll have two search planes in the air with the helicopter joining and climbers staged at the bottom to search pattern their way up the route. Okay, everybody, check over your gear, get some coffee, and do what you've got to do to get ready."

Forty-five minutes later, five climbers were snaking their way up the mountain, not talking, just moving.

Charlie thought about his friend, and his mind went back to all the incredible memories that bonded them forever. It was Spider who caught the touchdown passes delivered by Brenden's rocket arm. It was Brenden who got Charlie interested in Telemark skiing, that throwback to the original Norwegian downhill athletes. Brenden introduced Charlie to the girl he was going to marry, and Charlie had always been there to help Brenden study for tough exams during medical school.

How many days, he thought, *had they climbed and shared the beauty of the Colorado fourteeners?* He couldn't count. And now, his friend was somewhere up here, maybe hurt. Charlie's pace picked up even more as he considered the danger.

Arriving at the top, he found that he was right. Brenden had marked his route up the main couloir on the mountain manifest. That meant he may have fallen on the scree-slicked surface, and anything could have happened.

The team leader radioed down to base, and climbers began to work their way up as the hasty team started down, narrowing the field of possibility. The climbers began to hear the sound of the search planes and the helicopter as they worked their way down, their eyes scanning every nook and cranny, searching, ever searching.

The man on Charlie's left saw it first—a backpack Charlie quickly identified as Brenden's. It only took a few more minutes for the team to find the badly injured man. His breathing was shallow. He was unconscious, probably in a trauma-induced coma brought on by the bang on his head indicated by the broken climbing helmet.

At least a concussion, Charlie thought, *maybe brain trauma*.

Brenden's pulse fluttered, and his blood pressure was dropping. Though it was June, temperatures on the mountain were in the teens, and Brenden showed indications of early stages of hypothermia.

"We've got to get him down," the team leader said. "We've got to get him down in a hurry."

The call went out to the helicopter, but the pilot quickly decided that the angle was too difficult to risk a landing.

"We need the basket," the team leader radioed. "It's gonna be the hard way—climbing anchors and hand-over-hand—but we'll get him down to a flat area as quickly as we can. Then you Flight for Life guys can medevac him to Frisco, Denver, or Grand Junction."

"Grand Junction is standing by," the helicopter pilot radioed back. "Go easy. We're right here when you're ready."

Charlie grumbled. "IHOG rules. We're gonna waste a lot of time."

IHOG was the International Helicopter Operating Guidelines, and with all the accidents that occurred around the country, Flight for Life simply would not stretch the regulations. The team worked as fast as it could, with the paramedic assigned to Brenden constantly checking the young man's vital signs.

Forty-five minutes later they found the flat spot, and five minutes after that Brenden and Charlie were on their way to St. Mary's Medical Center in Grand Junction. The paramedics on board were feverishly working to warm Brenden with thermal blankets and gentle massage. Charlie took the time to call Brenden's mother and alert her that they had found her son and where they were going.

"Thank you, Charlie, thank you," she said. "I'll start driving to Grand Junction right now."

The pilot interrupted. "Tell the guy's mom that after we drop him off, we'll pick her up. My office will call her and tell her where to be."

"That's awesome," Charlie said, and he passed the information on to Mora.

Over the next twenty minutes, Charlie alternated between watching his friend and praying, something he hadn't done a lot of, but something he very much hoped God would hear.

chapter five

Smitty. Smitty. Smitty.

The black Lab stood in the backseat of the car, shaking as if he were on point, hunting birds. Then he began to turn in circles—off the seat to the floor, back up again, down again, back up. When the driver came around and opened the car door, the dog leaped forward, nearly taking the man holding the leash off his feet.

"Okay, Bart, okay." Dan laughed. "I know. That's your Smitty. Go ahead, boy. Go ahead."

By now, Harold Smith had reached the bottom of the stairs. He dropped to his knees, opening his arms to receive the animal, whose heart pounded so hard it could be felt through his skin. It was hard to tell at that moment who was happier—the man or the dog.

Neither of them expected this moment ever to happen. As his trainer, Smitty wanted Bart to succeed in the field, and the animal accepted his new life and responsibility in the fulfillment of his guide dog purpose not once, but twice. Now fate stepped in and brought these two friends back together in a reunion that was as deeply felt as could be imagined.

Smitty remembered that Bart had never really been a verbal animal—not a barker in the kennel or a dog that used his voice to express his feelings. But now the emotion poured out of the big black Lab, and he made high-pitched singing noises. He covered the man with kisses and tried desperately to climb into his arms. Failing that, he turned in circles, forcing Smitty to move his head out of the way every time the long tail whipped around. The dog rubbed his entire body against the man, and sounds of disbelief and excitement came from deep inside his chest.

Smitty was actually surprised when, despite himself, he became aware of a few tears falling from the corners of his own eyes.

"Do you want me to put him in the kennel, Smitty?"

"No, no, that's okay, Dan. I'll take care of it. Thanks for picking him up."

"What about the rest of the paperwork?" Dan asked. "Do you want me to fill it out?"

"Naw." Smitty laughed. "It's late. You've been driving all day. I'll take care of that in the morning."

"Okeydokey," Dan said. "I'll head on home. That's one happy dog right there. I don't know if I've ever seen one so glad to see his trainer. Good night, Smitty."

"Good night, Dan."

As the car pulled away, Smitty thought about what Dan had just said. Sitting on the steps still hugging the big dog, Smitty knew that this was more than the usual dog/ex-trainer reunion. He really crossed the line with this animal. Oh sure, he loved all the dogs he worked with, but somehow this behaviorally challenged friend reached the part of his heart that made him willing to break every rule in order to make sure Bart would have a great life.

"Okay, pal," he said, rising. "Somehow we're going to have to figure out how to check you back into school, so I think I'll take you home for a few days while we think about it. How do you feel about that?"

The big dog nuzzled his hand, making it clear he didn't care what they did—he was with Trainer, so anything was just fine with him.

The man and the dog found Smitty's Camaro in the parking lot, and in a few minutes they were on the highway headed home.

Bart still trembled with excitement as he settled on the seat next to Smitty, within reach of his hand. He didn't take his eyes off the man, and the black tail thumped every time Smitty glanced his way. Bart didn't understand how all this had happened, and he didn't care.

For his part, the man was aware that he had a real problem.

There were many things that Smitty didn't know much about, but he had come to realize one thing. Although he could never admit it publicly, with very few exceptions he liked—no, *loved*—dogs more than he liked most people.

After fifty years on the planet, there were some basic truths he understood. A dog's love was absolute and did not require anything but love honestly given in return. He was convinced that there were no bad dogs, only those that were misunderstood or mishandled by the humans they interacted with. He knew the viable communication possible with these creatures simply by paying attention and learning to read their body language and tone of voice, just as they read his.

Smitty developed all of these feelings and many ingrained instincts over thirty years as a professional trainer, first in the air force, where he worked with rescue dogs, and later on a tenure with the Detroit PD with drug enforcement animals. It was good fortune that brought him into guide dog work, where he had placed over a thousand teams of dogs and blind people into the field. There was no question that Smitty loved what he did, and if he were really honest with himself, he would have to admit that he was obsessed with his work and the dogs that he trained.

This obsession, he knew, had cost him his marriage. He could even remember the night when it hit the fan. His wife accused him of loving animals more than he loved her, and in that moment of real candor, he realized that she was probably right.

Since then he had lived as a confirmed bachelor in a two-bedroom basement apartment without much of a view. He slept in one of the bedrooms, and the other became his designated hall of fame with walls filled to bursting with pictures of dogs and people, the teams he was so proud of. His two indispensable possessions dominated his living room: a large La-Z-Boy chair and his one true luxury—a gigantic plasma screen TV that cost him a fortune.

Smitty was a sports junkie, and along with never missing a good game, he wasn't averse to betting on a few that he thought were stone-cold lead pipe locks. Thankfully he never bet a lot. He learned that he just couldn't pick 'em. In fact, there were some months when he cut back on his beer budget to pay off his losses.

This was his favorite time of year, when the Giants were getting ready for spring training, the NBA's Warriors were laboring in the middle of another losing season, and the 49ers prepared for the NFL draft in the hope that they would find the next Rice or Montana. He was thankful that ESPN covered the rest of the country, because a sports junkie never knew when he might wake up at three in the morning and just have to see the national highlights.

IF HOME IS WHERE THE heart is, Smitty's house was exactly where Bart wanted to be, even if it was the simple abode of a not-too-domestic bachelor.

The staccato beat of Bart's tail on the kitchen floor reflected the joy in his eyes as he watched Smitty moving about to build himself a big sandwich. The last few days had been the happiest in the dog's whole life. He was with Smitty. Not in a kennel, not in a house with people who didn't understand him, like Lady. He was here with the one he cared most about in the world, and that's all a dog really needed.

Smitty had to acknowledge he was just marking time, since he really didn't know what to do next. Beth was probably right: he couldn't keep checking Bart back into school as a beginning dog candidate. He had already broken all the very firm rules about not allowing more than two recycles of new masters for any dog. However, he was convinced that Bart was the best dog he had ever trained, and somehow he could not let this animal go without fulfilling his mission. Beyond that, Bart got to him on a deep emotional level, and Smitty knew he crossed professional lines when he allowed his heart to get involved.

He hated the idea that Bart had been rejected twice, and he had only himself to blame. He was the one responsible for matching Bart with the two men who had been his temporary masters. Looking back, he couldn't say either choice was ideal, but sometimes when a dog is ready to go, the perfect match doesn't come along. *That's the toughest part of all*, Smitty thought. *You can't keep these dogs hanging around until they're three or four years old, waiting for the right person—you want to get them active in the work while they're sharp. You tend to forget that some of those blind people aren't right for a guide dog in the first place.*

Smitty chuckled as he bit into his sandwich. *It's like an online dating service. The match may not be perfect, but sometimes the natural order of love and commitment will fill in the spaces. Sometimes. Not every time.*

Smitty continued to enjoy his sandwich, in spite of Bart's big dog eyes.

"Looks like your last master must have been feeding you from the table, boy. Bad idea. At least that's one rule we won't break."

Smitty understood completely that Bart was a lot of dog to handle. He thought of him like a precocious child—a genius when applying himself to the work, but a terror on four paws when he was off duty and tempted by food or things to chew or be curious about. At two and a half, he was like a teenager slow to develop maturity.

Looking into the bright eyes, Smitty was aware yet again that this fellow was something more. No dog he had ever trained grasped concepts so quickly. No animal was more aggressive or definite in his work when he made a decision. Yet no dog could be more loving, which was obvious every night when Bart collapsed next to him, taking up most of the double bed they shared.

Smitty reached a finger to scratch between those bright eyes fixed on him.

"I won't give up on you, my friend. If I ever manage to get you back in the field again, it will only be with somebody good enough to deserve you. And strong enough to handle you!"

It was halftime in the Lakers/Warriors basketball game, so Smitty put his plate and beer can in the sink and picked up the paperwork on the group of students who would be coming into his next class. The string of dogs that he presently worked was the J litter of that year, meaning that all of the names began with the letter J. As Smitty scanned them, reality dawned as to what the next step must be.

"Bart, my boy," he said, looking at the big animal on the floor whose tail responded immediately, "we have to change your name—one more time. Then we just might try to sneak you into the next string of dogs."

Smitty glanced back at the papers in front of him.

"When I finish this J class—let's see, uh—based on the number of trainers, I'll probably be getting the N litter. Okay. Who will you be?"

The tail wagged again.

"You're such a great guy. Even after a couple of masters, you're still an optimist. So what should we call you?"

On the big screen was a news update being given during the halftime break in the game. The anchor talked about Oprah Winfrey's contribution to South Africa. She recently provided over forty million dollars to develop a school for girls, and the news showed pictures of the opening ceremony. Smitty watched as Nelson Mandela, the revered leader of his people and Nobel Prize winner, helped Oprah cut the ribbon for the opening of the wonderful new school.

"That's it! Nelson!" Smitty clapped his hands, causing Bart to lift his head, curious at the sound. "Nelson," Smitty said again. "That's exactly who you're going to be. Bart, my boy, you're going to be Nelson."

The dog tipped his head and took on a quizzical look, trying to figure out what a Nelson was.

OVER THE NEXT FEW DAYS, he would find out. Smitty had done this before. Dogs, he knew, could adjust to a different name if it was introduced in the right way. The approach was to blend the monikers, so as the animal worked, Smitty would say, "Sit, Bart; down, Nelson," or "Come, Nelson; heel, Bart," and then gradually phase out the original name.

Over the next two weeks, that's exactly what the trainer did, and by day fifteen, Bart the black Lab converted to Nelson, a dog in the N string looking for a new master.

chapter six

When Mora got the call from Flight for Life telling her that she could be helicoptered to Grand Junction and St. Mary's Hospital, her first thought was what to do with Gus. He had a doggy door, and she could leave him with food, but she went next door and asked a friendly neighbor to keep an eye on him.

Then she picked up the phone and called Lindsey, not because she cared whether Lindsey was there or not, but because she felt the need to do what Brenden would have wanted. Lindsey mattered to Brenden. She mattered very much. And so Mora made the call.

Lindsey was already in class listening to a lecture on contracts. When her cell phone buzzed, she climbed over a few people to leave the room and answer it.

"Hello," she said, with a tinge of irritation in her voice.

"Lindsey? It's Mora, Brenden's mother. There has been an

accident, and they're bringing him down off the mountain to St. Mary's Hospital in Grand Junction. They've offered to helicopter me up there to save time. I thought you might want to come to the house and join me."

"That's horrible!" Lindsey said. "Is he all right? Do you know anything?"

"Charlie Evans is with the climbing team that found him. He says that Brenden is unconscious and probably suffering from a concussion or more severe head trauma. That's all I know at the moment. Can you get here quickly?"

The beat before Lindsey responded took a little too long.

"I think so. Yes. I can join you. I need to talk to a couple of professors. I mean, we're in the middle of midterms and everything."

Mora cut her off. "I can't wait for you, Lindsey. I'm going to go ahead, but I know Brenden would like you to be there as soon as possible when he wakes up. You know where St. Mary's is in Grand Junction? It's about a two-hour drive. Get there as quickly as you can."

Mora hung up, not giving the girl any time to respond.

Lindsey stood there, the cell phone in her hand, wondering why she hadn't just said, "I'll be right there, Mrs. McCarthy." Was she that selfish? The thought lit briefly in her mind and just as quickly flew out again. After all, she had been worried. In truth, she hadn't slept all night, wondering where Brenden was and if he was okay. She put those thoughts aside and returned to contract class, figuring to talk to her professors at the end of the hour and then head for Grand Junction.

DR. MARK JAMES, THE NEUROLOGIST on call for St. Mary's Hospital, hated being brought in on cases like this. A young guy unconscious with head trauma, they told him. Probably hemorrhaging. Probably bleeding somewhere into the brain. He arrived at the hospital before the helicopter landed and immediately ordered an MRI after the patient was stabilized.

On the first examination he knew right away that the patient was in trouble. He was clearly in shock with extremely low blood pressure. Everything pointed to a very dangerous situation, and the MRI didn't help. There was major bleeding in the occipital lobe of the brain, and he knew that they had to try and bring down the edema in the area. He didn't want to have to operate in that section of the brain. He knew from past experience that anything could go wrong. So for now he decided to try medications. Actually, steroids. He chose Decadron, knowing it was fast acting and time was essential.

This was the worst part of his job: the waiting. No, actually the worst part of his job was having to talk to families, which was exactly what he had to do now. A second copter brought the boy's mother to the hospital, and so, here they were in a stark waiting room with the doctor aware that he had very little comfort to offer.

Dr. James was struck by the quiet strength and poise he saw in the face of the woman sitting opposite him. *This is a woman*, he thought, *who has seen a lot in her life and, thank God, has good coping skills*. After explaining the injury and the immediate course of treatment for Brenden, the doctor was impressed with her next question.

"Dr. James," she asked, "the occipital lobe area of the brain, what does that—I mean, will this kind of injury affect Brenden's ability to think? Or maybe limit his movement? I mean paralysis? What are we talking about?"

The doctor took a deep breath. "Mrs. McCarthy," he said carefully, "this part of the brain controls the vision center."

The doctor saw the woman's hands begin to shake slightly as she leaned forward. "You mean, he could be—he could be—" Now her hands went to her face, as if she tried to hold back the words.

The doctor went on gently. "The truth is, Mrs. McCarthy, we won't know to what extent Brenden's sight will be affected until he comes out of the coma. Right now, we're using drugs to bring down the edema—the swelling on the brain. We simply don't have a clear picture of his prognosis. We know the occipital lobe has been affected, but there is no way to truly measure the extent of the damage. The truth is, we won't know until your son tells us himself."

The woman seemed to pull inside herself and then quietly asked, "You mean, he'll be blind?"

"It's possible, Mrs. McCarthy, but until we get the edema under control and induce Brenden's regaining consciousness, we simply don't know. I'm sorry that I can't be more specific, but in these cases, we basically have to take a wait-and-see approach."

Mora took a deep breath. "To see. I suppose that really is the question, isn't it, doctor?"

BRENDEN'S FIRST AWARENESS WAS OF movement and vibration. Then a jarring and the vibration stopped. Then motion again. He was being moved, his mind only taking in impressions, not thoughts. No clarity. Just snippets of perception. He fought the haze, then succumbed to it, fought again and then rested, each time moving a little closer to being aware, swimming to the surface. He could hear voices, but he could not understand what they were saying. He lay on a hard surface, and there was a repetitive banging sound. Was that in his head or from the outside?

Again he felt himself being moved, and the surface became soft. He felt the needle in his arm but only registered it as a slight sense of pain and then nothing, as he rested again. Each time he tried to climb out of the haze, the monumental effort seemed as impossible as Everest. He wanted to be in the world, but getting there—it was so hard to get there.

AFTER WORKING THINGS OUT WITH her professors, Lindsey Reynolds broke every speed limit as she rocketed toward Grand Junction. She refused to consider whether it was competitive adrenaline or guilt that drove her. But as in everything she did, she was in full concentration, driven to the max by whatever motivated her.

Thankful that she hadn't been stopped by the highway patrol, she skidded into the parking lot of St. Mary's after an hour and thirty-seven minutes. As she entered the hospital, she noticed Charlie Evans's beat-up Ford truck already there. She found the waiting room and joined the watch-and-wait group.

Not long after she arrived, Dr. James came out and told

them that he was pleased. Twenty-four hours passed with the patient still unconscious, but a second MRI indicated that the edema was coming down. On further examination, the patient's eyes were beginning to flutter, and involuntary muscle spasms suggested definite neurological activity. All very good signs.

NOW BRENDEN COULD HEAR PEOPLE talking, and words began to take shape, though he could not yet quite connect them into sentences. He could feel the warmth of the sheets and smell—what was that smell? He remembered. *Hospital*. The days with his father. It was a hospital smell. And now yesterday came back: the mountain and the fall. His head banging down the rock face. *No! No!* He thought he screamed and then knew he hadn't. He willed himself this time not to move upward but to sink back into the quiet. *Sleep. To sleep*. He wanted to sleep, but someone wouldn't let him. Hands gently shook him. Voices were becoming even more clear.

"He's coming around," someone said. "Wake him up. Come on, people. Wake him up."

All right, he thought reluctantly, *let's wake up. I can hear everyone, but where are they? My eyes. Let me rub my eyes.*

Slowly, slowly, Brenden's right hand began to move, and the people in the room saw it with a surge of hope.

"Brenden? Brenden?" Mora said, leaning even closer to the bed. "Brenden, are you awake?"

His hand reached his eyes and rubbed them.

"Mother? Mom? Is that you?"

"Yes, dear," Mora said softly, "I'm right here. Charlie's here, too, and Lindsey."

He could smell Lindsey's perfume and heard Charlie cough. But where were they?

He croaked the words out. "I can't—I can't—see you. You're here. All of you are here, but I can't see you."

"Brenden, I'm Dr. James."

Someone took his hand.

"You've had a pretty bad bang on the head, and it may have affected the occipital lobe. Can you understand me?"

The occipital lobe. Brenden struggled to work his way out of the haze and grasp what he was told. "The occipital— The occipital— I can't see anyone. The occipital—lobe."

"Yes, that's right," the doctor's voice said. "It's the area of the brain that governs vision."

The thought seared through the haze of his concussed state. It was as sharp and clear as an electrical current. It exploded in his head like a bolt of lightning and expressed itself in a cry so guttural, so basic in its primitive pain, that no one in the room who heard it ever forgot it.

"I can't see! I can't see! I'm blind! Blind! Bl—ind!!"

The shot quickly administered by a nurse who had seen this before sent Brenden back into blessed sleep.

Dr. James looked at the people in the room.

"I hate to do that when he's concussed, but with the bleeding going on, we can't have him upset. That kind of agitation could cause additional hemorrhaging. I'm sorry, but we're going to have to put him in restraints."

Lindsey gasped audibly, and Mora clutched the rails of the bed.

"No," she said, "Dr. James, you don't have to do that. We'll monitor Brenden. We'll keep him relaxed."

"I don't think so," the doctor said quietly. "You all need to understand that this is not just simple vision loss. It isn't temporary. Your son had it right. Barring a miracle, he's going to be permanently blind."

chapter seven

Dark. Darkness. I will forever live in a state of darkness. To be blind means to live in the dark. To never see the light. To never know a sunrise. Never see color—the gold of the aspens in the fall; the blue of the ocean; the reds, yellows, purples, and oranges. To never see a sunset. Being blind is to never see a smile or to see my Lindsey's eyes when they dance at the pleasure of a joke I've told.

I am blind. I won't live like this. I can't live *like this. Life, my life isn't worth living if it's going to be like this, if I'm going to exist in a constant state of darkness, never being able to see the light.*

Brenden McCarthy thought all of these things as the reality of his situation began to replace the haze of concussion. He tried to sleep to blank out the pain of his thoughts, but the pain was overwhelming, and it enveloped him in an impenetrable blanket of self-pity. No one could touch him. Love could not breach the walls he built up.

Already he had constructed a personal identity that said he would never be a doctor, and he would never treat patients. He would never even be able to care for himself. He would be forever helpless, dependent, worthless, handicapped, blind. From Superman with super thoughts and dreams, hopes and ideas, Brenden had become Clark Kent—invisible, vacuous, disconnected—and all of this occurred in an accident that took only five seconds.

He expressed none of these emotions. Time had not yet allowed him to come to terms with his feelings, much less to communicate them, and so he did not speak. Not to his mother, who constantly sat at the end of his bed, or to Charlie, who hovered at the far side of the room, or to Lindsey. He registered that Lindsey came and went, like a restless bird, not willing to perch or nest.

He registered this information but did not indicate he knew. He worked to keep his eyes closed, pretending to be asleep, wanting to remain alone. He heard their muffled conversations, wondering oddly if his newly acquired blindness already improved his capacity to listen. They spoke quietly, sometimes with each other in shorthand and sometimes with the doctor, a good man who came in twice a day to check on him.

When that man asked him how he was doing, the manners that his mother had so diligently worked to teach him instinctively took over. He said he was fine, that nothing hurt, that he wanted to go home as soon as possible, and then when the doctor left, he would turn his face to the wall, especially after the physician confirmed to all of them that the damage to the occipital lobe, causing his blindness, would quite likely be permanent. Surprisingly, they did not press him. In fact, they, too, seemed uncomfortable about sharing any conversation that would open up the floodgates to feelings so new and not yet understood.

He heard them discussing the preparations they were making with the hospital's rehab people regarding what they might do to make his homecoming easier. They would be signing him up for adult classes in mobility and rehabilitation. His mother talked about finding a counselor who would help him begin to move forward with his life. Charlie even talked about things that they could still do together.

Brenden heard it all, absorbed it, and then threw it all away. He was blind, and that meant life was over. Oh sure, he had read about people like Helen Keller, who overcame her double disability; Stevie Wonder and Ray Charles, who were remarkably gifted in music; and there was even this guy, Eric Weihenmayer, who recently climbed Mount Everest. But they weren't Brenden McCarthy, and he wasn't willing even to try to get his life back. What was the point? God had dumped him on that mountain, and so he would quit, give up.

Lying there in his hospital bed, the weight of his situation crushing his chest, crushing his heart, he was sure that God would not punish him for wanting to escape. Wasn't it God who had caused his injury? And so shouldn't God cut him a little slack, forgive him for his sin and grant him his place in heaven?

Visiting hours finally ended, and the blessed night settled over the hospital. He was so glad his mother and Charlie had gone back to the motel and he was alone. And where was Lindsey? He didn't know, and his recognition that she wasn't there profoundly deepened his sense of hopelessness and self-pity.

Time moved slowly because he was unable to sleep, and in that state he found himself unable to shut off his mind. For the hundredth time, he considered how he could bring his now worthless life to an end. He wished that his head had split wide open in the fall. He so wished that he had died that way, certainly causing his mother grief, but nowhere near as much as she would feel when he acted on the decision he knew he was going to make.

How to end it, he thought. *How to rid the world of a useless young man with an infirmity. How to check out of my personal existence.*

The limitations of his blindness reduced his choices, even in this ultimate act. He knew from listening to conversations that he was on the second floor of the hospital, probably not high enough to jump, even if he could find and then open a window. There were no pills available, and nothing sharp within his reach. So what did all that mean? He would have to go home and work on his demise from there. And yet that wouldn't be right. It wouldn't be fair to his mother. No. He would have to create an alternative, and that would require him to at least tacitly begin some kind of rehabilitation process, even if it only meant that it got him out of his house and into a different environment. So tomorrow he would go home, and then he thought of a phrase that almost made him laugh. He would keep his eyes open—*ha!*—until he found the opportunity to—*what*? He knew the inevitable answer to that question.

How many days had it been? Mora wondered as Charlie drove her back to the motel where they had been staying. She actually couldn't remember. Time ceased to exist, and like her son, day and night did not seem to have any significance. The world turned, but hers stopped. She had buried her husband, and now what? What did the fates—or more relevant to her, faith—really mean? What did God have in mind? What test was she expected to cope with now? What was she supposed to learn?

After thanking Charlie and closing the door to her room, she flopped onto the bed and buried her face in the pillows. She wanted to scream. She wanted God to hear. She wanted him to know how unfair it all was. *I could cope with Brian's death*, she thought, *but my son being blind; I don't know if I can handle that. More to the point, I don't know if he can. Or even more to the point, I don't know if he has the will.*

Her thoughts somehow became a prayer. *Dear God, please give Brenden the strength to understand the way and to accept his burden as your will. Amen.* Like a hamster on a wheel, the thought kept revolving—the same prayer over and over again.

Over the last few days, she had done what she always did—jump into any crisis and try to become organized. She had talked to the Colorado Rehabilitation Center for the Blind and been referred to a counselor in Denver, who surprised her when he spoke by telling her that Brenden's reaction was not particularly unusual.

"There has to be a grieving period," he said, "and from what little I know about your son, there also has to be some time to allow anger to be expressed. Stabilizing him psychologically will take time, Mrs. McCarthy. It's a long road with a great many pitfalls, but we'll work on it together, one step at a time."

"Is there anything I should be doing? I mean, in terms of preparing our house for his coming home?"

The man on the other end laughed softly. "I'm sorry, Mrs. McCarthy. I didn't mean to laugh. It's just that people ask me that all the time. What's most important for your son and for any newly blind person is that everything in his surroundings be the same as he remembers when he was sighted. We'll be trying to plug his new, developing sensory capacity and mobility into the mental pictures of environments that he already had before his accident."

"Thank you," Mora said, understanding. "I'll just try to make it like home."

"That's worth a lot, Mrs. McCarthy. Love is always the best cure-all."

LINDSEY HAD BEEN IN AND out of the hospital for the last three days, and as she drove home to Denver, this time obeying the speed limits, she was angry at herself. Why had she been so uncomfortable with Brenden and his mother? *Of course I'm worried*, she thought. *I love Brenden. I want him to get well, to see again. Is that it? Am I so selfish that if he's not perfect, I can't handle it? Do I not have the patience or goodness or love to share my life with someone who*—she nearly choked on the words—*is handicapped?*

She pulled her car into a rest stop as the tears started to come. Were they tears of sadness or tears of disgust at the kind of person she was being forced to face? Eventually, she shook off her malaise and framed her own reality. *It isn't wrong*, she thought to herself. *I'm not wrong if I'm not sure I can cope with this. I have hopes and dreams and goals of my own. If I can't handle the idea that someone I wanted to marry is going to be blind, that doesn't make me a bad person. Almost anyone with a life to live would feel the same way.*

Her cell phone buzzed.

"Lindsey? It's Andrea. Are you going to make study group? We really need your precedent brief."

Lindsey was glad for the diversion.

"I'll be there," she said. "Tell everyone not to worry. Lindsey the litigator will be there."

That's who she was going to be: a lady lawyer litigator, driven to be a lioness in court, a winner in life, and a woman with an unswerving determination to be the best.

BRENDEN WAS BACK AT HOME and in his bedroom. Another day. Another night. He didn't care. Nature was challenging his bladder, and he knew he had to deal with it. Earlier they had wheeled him out of the hospital, a requirement of the medical protocol, right to his mother's car, so all he had to do was get in and ride.

Arriving home, Charlie nearly carried him up to his room, both of them feeling completely awkward, not understanding how to move together. The newly blinded young man was hesitant to put one foot in front of the other, and his friend treated him as if he were a crystal vase. At last his mother kissed him good night and went to bed, and now he would have to make his first independent voyage.

Where was the bathroom? he thought, trying to picture it. *Out the door, down the hall, to the right.* That's what he remembered. Hands out in front of him, he moved hesitantly toward the door, but his angle was wrong, and he knocked a picture off his bureau—a picture of Lindsey, he knew—beautiful, independent, wonderful Lindsey. He hadn't heard from her today. That didn't really surprise him.

Finding the knob, he stepped into the hall and turned left. One, two, three, four, five steps. The door to the bathroom should be on his right. Extending his hands, the feeling of the mountain returned. His toes rocked over the edge, and he teetered precariously on the stairway.

Instinct took over as he fought to maintain his balance, throwing himself backward. He slid down the first three stairs on his rear and stopped. Gus got to him first. He loved this little dog, and the animal's concern immediately registered as he licked Brenden's face. His mother was right behind.

"Oh my— Brenden! Are you all right?"

"Oh sure," he said quickly. "I'm fine. Sorry, Mom. I guess I just turned the wrong way and forgot to turn the light on."

Neither one of them laughed at his effort to make a joke.

His mother helped him to the bathroom and then back to his bedroom, and for the first time in his life, Gus stayed with him, crawling up under the covers and snuggling close.

"Hey, Gus," Brenden said, "what are you going to do, become a seeing-eye dog? I think you're a little small for the work."

The dog licked him again.

"You know what?" Brenden told the animal in the dark. "You shouldn't waste your time on me. I'm not worth it, and I'm not going to be around for very long."

The animal cuddled into the man's shoulder, making it clear that he didn't agree.

chapter eight

By late-night stealth, a dozen roses for his secretary, and forged paperwork, Smitty once again enrolled Nelson, aka Bart, into the guide dog program. And the animal reluctantly took his place in the kennel with dogs on a string that were in stage three. Smitty hoped against hope for a student in his next class who would have the skills and drive to handle this most special animal. For now he would work Nelson as a part of his string and say a small prayer.

Smitty loved training guide dogs. He loved it because he felt it was the highest form of human-animal bonding. He also loved it because he knew that these remarkable creatures gave without question once they committed to their masters. "Love in its purest form," he always told friends. "That's what we see when we work with these dogs, love in its purest form."

He learned the history of guide work when he came into the

field after his years in the air force. The work began in Germany at around the turn of the century and found its way to America just after World War II. A remarkable woman named Dorothy Eustis became aware of young German soldiers blinded during the war who were using dogs as guides. She had the vision to bring the work to America, and over the years her work changed the lives of countless blind people across the country.

When he became a guide dog trainer, Smitty learned that only three out of every hundred canine candidates found their way into the work. Today with the scientific sophistication of excellent breeding programs and puppy raisers who teach basic socialization and obedience skills, that ratio had improved dramatically. Smitty was delighted that six or seven out of every ten dogs who made it through the difficult training process now went on to take their places with blind people around the world. He so admired the people who were willing to be those puppy raisers. These were the best of the best, as far as he was concerned—human beings who poured their hearts into the animals during their first crucial months and then gave them up to a higher calling. True, Smitty also had to endure the same parting when he completed his work with an animal, but somehow the civilians, as he thought of them, really deserved a lot of credit.

His string began its third stage of training, and, as always, he was behind in his paperwork. The animals were graded on a one-to-five scale, with no dog going into the field that didn't score a three or above on every criterion of behavior. So as Smitty labored to complete his overdue report on the animals, he considered the training cycle the dogs were going through.

First and foremost, all of the animals who arrived at Guide Dogs for the Blind had to become comfortable in kennel life. They had been living with families, and all of them hated the restriction of the kennel. So in the first few days of association with their new handler, a whole lot of TLC had to be doled out, and the dogs generally responded gratefully to the love.

Smitty always looked for patterns in the animals as he worked to reinforce the basic obedience instilled by the puppy raisers. *Sit*, *down*, *stay*, *come*, and *let's go*, a more informal way of suggesting the traditional *heel*. He always watched the dog's eyes for any hesitation or fear or to see if the dog was too sensitive when given gentle suggestion or correction. Smitty also looked for any extended lapses of attention as the dogs interacted with other dogs in the string.

He sat at his desk reviewing his notes on Nathaniel, a yellow Lab with much the same personality as Nelson. Nathaniel loved it when they employed the new technique of treadmilling the dogs. Treadmilling occurred the first few days after the animals got to know their trainers and enjoyed working through simple obedience. It was critical to the overall success of the work to create in the dog the desire to move forward in a straight line while maintaining a forward pressure in the harness. With that forward press, the blind master would be able to read every nuance of the dog's motion. This technique was called "harness pull," and it was critical if the dogs were ever going to perform appropriately in the field.

Using a treadmill and treats, the dogs would be encouraged—first for only fifteen to twenty seconds, and then eventually up to five minutes—to keep up with the pace of the treadmill, with the handler holding the harness. In this way the dog both felt the pressure of the harness on his chest and received rewards for maintaining his forward momentum.

Smitty was amazed at how well the use of the treadmill improved the way the dog translated his behavior to later work. Also, Smitty loved the idea that early in the training the dog and his new handler were having a sort of adventure that they both enjoyed.

Nathaniel did very well on his treadmill experience, and Smitty turned the page to take a look at Nathaniel's response to the next phase of training. This was called "pattern training."

The dogs spent about four weeks with their instructors literally patterning every behavior that would eventually be part of the real work. The catch was that none of it involved the use of the harness. The dogs were only asked to walk with their trainers and encouraged to understand the patterns that were presented.

During this four-week period, trainers provided the dog with every answer. They made sure that the animal moved in a straight line, avoided obstacles, stopped appropriately at the edge of curbs, and entered buildings safely. There was also the search for elevators and escalators, along with finding an empty chair or a car in a crowded parking garage. Then there were the overhangs. These were the most difficult obstacles to teach any animal, and instructors spent a lot of time reaching up and rattling the potential danger with their hands and encouraging the dogs to look up. In this process of positive conditioning, the animals were being exposed to the work they would eventually have to do for real with the blind people they would serve.

Smitty made a note in the margin that Nathaniel was one of those very good ones that seemed to take on the behaviors, even during this first month. He stopped at curbs on his own and even seemed willing to pick up his pace—"hop up" as they called it—whenever the trainer wanted the dog to move faster. He also noted that Nathaniel was a "little doggy," meaning that he could be distracted by other animals they passed in the street, not a good thing in guide work but certainly correctable.

In the second month of the animal's training, Smitty was amazed when he thought of how much positive reinforcement came out of the first four weeks, when the handler provided the animal with all the answers. As an example, Nathaniel moved immediately in a straight line when the harness was put on, maintaining constant pressure and providing the handler with good harness feel. He also stopped on a dime whenever they came upon a curb, though he still demonstrated a certain affinity to being "doggy."

One of the most complex issues facing dog and trainer is that of traffic check. For Smitty, this was critical in training any animal. He constantly reminded himself that dogs were color-blind and that their relationship to traffic motion needed to be a constant process of conditioning to the idea of danger.

Even in the early stages, when an instructor took all the responsibility for teaching the animal, dogs were encouraged to be acutely aware of traffic. Trainers conditioned and tested their dogs with a sort of game. Every time a car came close or sped around a corner, the dog would be asked to go forward, and then firmly but with love the idea was imposed that the dog was to stop in spite of the forward command.

In the entire training process, the positions of go and stop had to be handled carefully. And as Smitty reviewed the notes on Nathaniel, he was pleased to see that nothing disturbed the dog's sense of well-being. Actually, Smitty had refined this technique over the years by never applying the word *no* to the stop. He found that if he just used gentle physical restraint, the dogs got the idea.

Smitty read on. Nathaniel held up very well during the second month, in which the same first-month patterns of training were reapplied, this time with the trainer working the dog in the harness. At the end of the second month, all the instructors went under blindfolds when they worked their animals as a sort of final examination of the dog's development.

Smitty had mixed feelings about this idea. The simple truth was that no sighted person putting on a blindfold functioned in the way that a student would who had been blind since birth or over an extended period of time. On the other hand, Smitty rationalized that in many ways the dogs had to work harder to compensate for their instructors' ineptness than they would when they took their place in the field with a real blind person. In the end, he decided that blindfolding was an appropriate exercise.

This marked the halfway point in the training process. The third stage was probably the most critical in the transformation of the dogs. Here the animal was asked to demonstrate intelligent disobedience, and this was where Nathaniel scored remarkably well. The theory was that the dog must be willing to countermand the command of the trainer for the sake of safety. Forward only meant forward when it was safe, because traffic, an overhang, bad footing, manholes, or any other obstacle might threaten the safety of the blind person.

Smitty was always amazed at the capacity of the dogs to love enough so that even if they were aggressively corrected by the master because the blind person did not understand what was going on, the dog would hold firm and never endanger his person.

It was also in this period that the trainers developed their dog's work inside buildings. They took trips into San Francisco, where the dogs were forced to face extraordinary complexity in traffic patterns and people movement. When the animal freely took on the concept of intelligent disobedience, a working bond was truly complete. Smitty loved watching dogs gain in confidence, becoming ever happier as they took on more and more direct responsibility.

He loved to see an animal work with bright eyes and a constantly wagging tail, as if the dog was doing the thing he had been designed for. It came down to this: when the dog was ready to meet his blind master, the animal had to have the confidence to compensate for the hesitance and awkwardness that new students often exhibited. That confidence was critical to being able to grow and work together.

Trainers like to say everything comes down the leash, meaning that in the beginning the dog absolutely knows his job; it's the student who struggles. The turnaround happens as the student gains confidence and provides the animal with the kind of direction that allows them to become one—a team together.

Smitty knew that students came to the program in all sizes, shapes, and ages. He understood that his job was to make sure that the dogs were completely confident and ready to take on any concerns that might be expressed by their new handlers.

Smitty sat back in his chair thinking about Nathaniel's future. It was clear that this animal would do extremely well in the field if Smitty could match him appropriately. The key to good matching was to make the connection between student and dog, based on the animal's sensitivity along with the student's lifestyle, desire, and capacity to get the most from the animal. This balancing of dog and person was the most important part of what Smitty did.

As he sat reading Nathaniel's report, he couldn't help but think about Nelson. Over the last few days, he had taken the black Lab out of the kennel and worked him, astounded at the animal's talent. No dog he had ever known demonstrated the immediate awareness for the work that he felt in the handle of the harness when Nelson did his thing. This was simply the best dog he'd ever known, and as he looked at the list of students that would be coming and meeting the N class of guide dogs, he hoped to God there would be someone who could both handle and get the most from this astounding creature.

chapter**nine**

The secretary informed Brenden that Mr. Barnes would see him in just a few minutes after he finished a conference down the hall. Brenden sat uncomfortably on the edge of a couch, listening to the sound of a clock ticking in the far corner of the room and wondering how much time he'd have to spend with this intake counselor.

Charlie brought him to the offices of the Colorado Rehabilitation Center for the Blind for this required meeting. Brenden decided he would answer this guy's questions and make the session as quick as possible. He knew what he was going to do. This was just a formality. Nothing would change his plans.

In the three weeks since his accident, he rarely came out of his bedroom. In fact, his mother brought him most of his meals on a tray. Until this morning, he remained unshaven and just barely clean. Lindsey had been by to see him only twice, and on other days she made excuses that her workload was extremely heavy. The inevitability of where their relationship seemed to be heading deepened his depression. And so he was sure that nothing this man could say would make any difference.

The big voice from outside the door seemed to vibrate everything in the room.

"Annie, is the McCarthy kid here?" It sounded more like a pronouncement than a question.

"Waiting in your office, Mr. B."

Instantly, the door banged open, and Brenden heard the sound of an uneven step as he felt the floor shake under the big man's weight. The guy was on top of him before he could stand up.

"Welcome to Blinky University," the big man boomed, extending his hand and finding Brenden's, engulfing it in a massive shake that made Brenden, a good-sized guy himself, feel like a dwarf. "Welcome to the place where eyes open and lives are changed! I'm Marvin Barnes. They call me 'Bad News.' Sit down. Sit down. Sorry I'm late. The conference ran long, and it takes me a little while to move on this bad knee. They say I need surgery, but I really don't want it. I figure I'll be back skiing in a month. That's how I hurt it—up in Winter Park. You know, 280-pound former defensive tackles really shouldn't be letting gravity and inertia take them down steep hills at high speed. You can't fight gravity or age!"

While all this was happening, Brenden heard the big man move behind his desk and seat himself, his chair groaning in protest.

"You ski, McCarthy?"

"I used to," Brenden answered woodenly, "all the time."

"Well, good," Barnes said. "I'm on the racing team at Winter Park, and we need new blind skiers for the World Championships in a couple of years."

Brenden came to attention. "Excuse me?" he asked. "You mean you're—"

Barnes interrupted. "Blind? You bet, kid! Blind as a bat and black to boot! What a combo."

Barnes hit a button, and Brenden heard a synthetic voice coming through a couple of speakers he figured were probably on a computer on the man's desk.

"Ten thirty intake appointment with Brenden McCarthy, age twenty-five, practicing physician doing his internship, newly blind, hurt in a mountain climbing accident up on the Bells." Barnes hit the stop button.

"Is that about right, Brenden? Are those the basic facts?"

"Yes," Brenden said in a flat tone.

"Well, your mother and your friend, Charlie, tell me you've been hanging out in your room, feeling sorry for yourself. Is that about it?"

Brenden felt the color rise in his face, and the anger began to bubble up inside him like a volcano about to blow.

"Who are you to say that?" he asked defiantly. "We don't even know each other, and you're already judging me, like you have all the information about who I am or what I feel?"

The chair indicated that the man sat back. "That's good," he said. "Very good. At least I know that you can get emotional. If

I can get a rise out of you, that's the right first step. Now we just have to channel it. What do you know about being blind, Brenden, beyond that it means your eyes don't work?"

The clocked ticked off a few more seconds.

"It means that life sucks." Brenden spit out the words. "It means that I'll never be able to enjoy the things that have always brought me pleasure in life. It means that I won't have independence. It means that people will pity me. It means that I have to give up my career in medicine. It means that I'll probably be caning chairs or selling pencils or something like that. Isn't that what all of you do? Or maybe I'll become musical—tune pianos. How about that?"

The big man laughed quietly. "You know the guy who won the blind World Championships as a downhill skier went faster than Jean-Claude Killy did in the 1964 Olympic Games? Do you know that there's an amputee who holds many speed records for freeform skiing? Have you read about Eric Weihenmayer—the guy who climbed Mount Everest—or what about the blind people who become judges, senators, lawyers? There's even a fellow named David Hartman in Baltimore who is a practicing psychiatrist. He's got a medical degree like you, doesn't he? You can do all those things, Brenden, if you simply decide you want to. And if you want to, we'll give you all the training you need.

"And then there's something else. You'll learn that a life in the dark can open up levels of sensory awareness that you would never have believed possible. Talk about your mountains? I don't just go there in the winter to ski. I enjoy mountain bike riding in the summer on the back of a tandem with some poor soul driving on the front, working much too hard to pedal my fat self up and down the hills. And while I'm up there, I listen to meadowlarks and mountain streams. Things I might not have taken in before. You know what, kid? I've even heard deer running free and the trumpeting of elk in the fall during mating season. I've sat on a rock and enjoyed the best ham and cheese sandwich I've ever eaten in my life. Did you ever notice that food tastes a lot better at fourteen thousand feet?"

Brenden couldn't help but smile, and the big man heard it.

"I just heard you smile, young fella, and it's a wonderful sound. Give me five."

The giant reached over the desk and once again engulfed Brenden's hand, this time pumping it up and down for emphasis.

"What did you get out of that handshake, kid? What did it tell you?"

Despite himself, Brenden thought about it. "It says you ought to be a politician. It says you're trying to impress me with a lot of bravado about the beauty of blind. It tells me you're a cheerleader for the disabled of this world. And I'm not buying any of it."

The big man returned to his chair. "Okay, kid," he went on after a sigh. "I get the feeling you not only feel sorry for yourself, but you figure you're the only person on earth who ever got a bad break. Is that right?

"So here's my story. I moved to Colorado because I was the number one draft choice for the Denver Broncos, but there was also something going on called Vietnam that involved another draft. Getting picked by the NFL didn't stop Uncle Sam from sending my black hulk overseas. It was 1973, and with a little bit of luck, I would still have been playing when the guys began to get the big money. Yes siree, I would have been with John Elway and all the boys in the Super Bowl. And then there was a little matter of a mine blowing up in my face up by the DMZ, and it changed everything. I was kind of ugly before it went off in my mug. But now"—he laughed again—"now it's just as well you can't see because the scarring will never heal."

"Sorry," Brenden heard himself say. "I'm very sorry."

"You know what?" the man went on, "the scarring inside, well, that's healed pretty well. I'm quite a minority in this country—a 280-pound African-American blind guy with a wife and three kids, a house in suburbia that I can't pay for, and some bills that are overdue. All in all, I'm a pretty lucky son of a gun, don't you think?"

Brenden couldn't help it. He became absorbed by the man's honesty, drawn in by his openness. "Listen," he asked, "do you really like your life? I mean, the way it is? No bull? You're really okay about it?"

Brenden heard the big man lean forward, the desk creaking under the weight of his elbows. "Listen, Brenden," he said with sincerity in his tone, "you're in for a rocky road if you decide to try and take your place back in the world. Let me give you some statistics. There are a million and a half blind people in this country. Let's say out of that group there are about eight hundred thousand folks who could hold meaningful jobs. Yet only about 20 percent of us work. The rest of us, well, we live on the public dole, either because we haven't got the confidence or because we're simply lazy. You have to decide which one of those you want to be. Not many of us get married and have families, but frankly that's usually because we're much too focused on ourselves. A lot of us get involved in organizations for the blind. Not bad, but many of these organizations, well, frankly, they're pretty militant, and they become sanctuaries for angry human beings.

"In my own case, before I took this job, I spent ten years working on the outside just to prove I could. You'll still go through a lot of patronizing. You'll sit in a restaurant with some good friends some night, and a waitress will walk up to the table and say to them, 'What would he like to eat?' People will talk loud because they think that being deaf is also part of being blind. I suppose you can blame old Helen Keller for that.

"You'll get up some mornings, and if you're not well organized, you'll walk out of your house dressed like somebody left a rainbow in your closet. And a lot of times people will talk about you as if you're not really there. If you get lucky and get married and have kids, you'll probably get hit in the head with a baseball trying to coach Little League. And unless you're willing to work real hard here at the Center, you'll probably be eating frozen dinners or going out most of the time because you'll never really learn to cook. Are you getting what I'm saying, kid?"

Involuntarily, Brenden nodded, but before he could correct himself, Barnes interjected.

"I heard you nod. Starch in your collar. Got a girl, Brenden?" Barnes asked.

"Yeah—her name's Lindsey. She wants to be a lawyer."

"Well, here's the deal with relationships. If you find the right one, I mean someone who can really love you and appreciate you, your marriage can become even deeper because of the intimacy in the way you share. You'll read the newspapers together in the morning. You'll take walks at sunset holding hands. You'll listen when she's getting dressed to go out at night and know that she's making herself beautiful just for you. Your kids will be better off because they won't have any built-in prejudice.

"Blindness allows you to look past the labels and see life inside-out, rather than outside-in. Let me tell you something, kid—something I've really come to believe. Every disability can be turned into an ability if you want to make it that way. Now don't interrupt me. I know that doesn't seem true to you right now, but I'm telling you, you can count on it.

"If I had played in the NFL during the early seventies and gotten hurt, let's say in my second year, there was no insurance for players then or a pension to take care of us. I would have been a big black guy with beat-up knees and no real future."

"Okay," Brenden put in, "but you went to Vietnam and got all shot up. Are you telling me that's better?"

"No. That's not what I'm saying. What I'm telling you is that when God deals out a hand of cards, you have the ability to shuffle them any way you want. All of us can change our own destiny if we're willing to try. You have to decide if you're a glass-half-empty or a glass-half-full person. Let me ask you this, Brenden. What were you before your accident? I mean a month ago. Were you a glass-half-empty or a glass-half-full human being when you were climbing that mountain? How did you feel about yourself?"

Brenden thought for a minute, listening to the clock, this time taking even longer to answer the question. Finally in a soft voice, he said, "I was at the top of the world. Life was awesome. I had it all."

"Okay, kid," the man went on gently, "so what have you really lost?"

"I'm blind," Brenden answered, starting to tear up. "I'm blind!"

"That's right," Barnes said, "but you're still Brenden, and Brenden has a lot to offer life."

In a softer voice, Brenden said, "But not enough to offer Lindsey. I won't ever be enough for Lindsey."

"What?" Barnes said. "Speak up. Now I suppose I'm going deaf. What did you say?"

"Nothing," Brenden said. "Nothing. I was just talking to myself."

Barnes nodded but let it go and went on. "You know what I want it to say on my tombstone, Brenden, when I'm dead? 'Here lies big Marvin 'Bad News' Barnes—black man, husband, father, football player, veteran, activist, counselor, and friend, who, by the way, happened to be blind.' Listen to me, Brenden. I'm here for you. We're all here for you, and life is worth living if you just give it a chance."

The big man got to his feet and this time put his arm around Brenden's shoulder. "Listen, kid," he said, "I'm going to send someone in here to figure out what kind of a schedule you'll be on for classes. Over the next couple of months, you'll learn how to be independent, and I promise if you give it a shot, you'll feel like living again. It's this simple. Right now you believe that you'll always be dependent on someone else, and I suppose what I'm trying to do is get you to consider the idea that you can become independent. But the truth is, if your girl loves you and you have good friends, you'll learn that life is about being interdependent. And when you really get that idea into your head, being blind won't seem that important."

Brenden felt the warmth and power of the big man's hug and sagged back onto the couch.

"I'll give you a few minutes to collect yourself," Barnes said as he walked to the door. "Somebody will be in to see you in just a little while. Good luck, Brenden. I'll be right here for you—24-7. Okay, kid?"

After Barnes closed the door, Brenden sat very still, working to absorb the emotions he had just experienced. Was the man right? Could life take on meaning for him? Was there a possible light at the end of the tunnel?

The door opened, and a woman came in. She asked him a few questions and jotted notes on some kind of calendar or legal pad. In minutes, Brenden worked out a schedule and began a new chapter in his life.

chapter ten

Over the next few days before Brenden undertook his rehabilitation program, Barnes's magic began to wane in the face of doubt, anger, and depression. Doubt because he still experienced difficulty even with the simple navigation of his own house. True, he hadn't fallen down any stairs, but he occasionally got lost in the middle of his living room when he rose from a chair and found himself turned the wrong way.

Doubt created anger, an emotion that was never far from the surface of his consciousness. And depression—well, depression was the natural spin-off from anger in those moments when he felt completely sorry for himself or missed Lindsey or hated the patronizing way his mother tried to be helpful.

He knew that she didn't mean any harm. She was simply being his mother. But his nerves were frayed to the breaking point, and even the smallest indication of patronage set him off, either into rage or into a pitiable state of sadness when he thought about his life circumstance.

It didn't make him any happier when on the first morning he was to report to rehab, the van provided by the program pulled up in front of his house, and he joined six other pathetic human beings headed for the place where they would be rehabilitated.

What a concept, he considered, as he sat morosely in the back row of the van. *Rehabilitation. To be rehabilitated.* That's what he was to become. *Reengineered. Reorganized. Reconstructed. Revamped. Renewed.* It was all garbage as far as he was concerned. Whatever you called it, to Brenden McCarthy it meant that he would never be the same free spirit he had once been and that his life, or what was left of it, would never be worth much to anyone, particularly to himself.

He learned that in this group of people riding to rehab, he was not particularly unusual. Two of his van-mates suffered from diabetes and just "had the lights go out," as they put it, in the last few months. Then there was a guy who had retinitis pigmentosa, a condition that brought him to blindness so gradually that he had gone into denial, unwilling to acknowledge and prepare for it. An older woman in the van had let macular degeneration go on too long, and by the time she finally went for treatment it was too late. And so all of them carried the same kind of symptomatic sorry that was eating him up inside.

Oh sure, he had been impressed with the stuff that Barnes talked about. And he had to admit that the big man seemed to be doing very well with his own adjustment. But he and Barnes weren't the same, and he just didn't believe that he would ever crawl out of the depths of his darkness and gain back the joy that had been so much a part of the person he used to be.

HIS DAYS BEGAN WITH MOBILITY training, another term that, to him, seemed deceptively innocuous. To Brenden—the mountain climber who could move from rock to rock with the surefooted agility of a cat—being limited to moving through space either holding on to the arm of a well-meaning instructor or trailing the wall in search of a door—well, this certainly didn't feel much like independence.

Counting steps and memorizing the simplest of routes to get from one destination to another required tremendous levels of concentration. He realized early on that his adjustment to a world in the dark would not come easily. That was expressed best in the frustration he experienced in the class the rehab people called living skills.

He figured out how to take someone's arm and understood how to move through space and read body motion. He found that his senses were picking up more information. But he always hated the use of the cane. Carrying a stick in his hands seemed pointless, and it didn't prevent him from bruising his shins or tripping on a step, hitting an overhang or getting lost on a planned route.

He didn't like most of the people who were in the program with him because they seemed old and tired, and he hated the fact that Lindsey wasn't around very much. He knew he would have to deal with her to win her back, to make her understand that he could succeed. But more importantly, he knew that he had to believe in that possibility himself, and he had not yet reached that place. Would he ever get there? He wasn't sure.

Brenden's thoughts of suicide were losing their urgency. They were still there but less of a preoccupation—more a plan B. He himself wasn't aware of the change.

Brenden had to admit that he was surprised at all the options available to blind people, helping them cope with every element of daily life.

He found himself reluctantly absorbed in the training. From learning to cook on a stove with voice-actuated timers to the use of the Kurzweil reading machine and JAWS software; the voice-actuated clocks that could be set by holding down buttons and listening while the chip moved the alarm to the time you wanted to get up. Then there was the question of finding the right clothes in the closet and working out a personal label system.

During this labeling process, Brenden was forced to begin learning Braille. It was soon obvious to him that this was a skill that would take a long time to perfect. Teaching your fingers to distinguish the Frenchman Louis Braille's touch code for letters and numbers was a slow, arduous process that carried with it incredible levels of frustration.

Consequently, most of the students either used stick-on dots placed in patterns that could be recognized by touch with an individual system of identification chosen by the students themselves, or by using a marvelous machine that was voice-actuated, called a talking color identifier.

This terrific little device was able to tell the listener the color of the garment. Brenden, not a particularly creative dresser, was pleased to be able to buy one of these units and organize his clothes in the appropriate color combinations. He learned to hang outfits together so that after a few weeks his closet was organized, and he was doing surprisingly well with his clothes.

Though he may have been dressed okay, his kitchen skills were woefully lacking. One of his most embarrassing moments occurred the first time he attempted to pour his own milk and forgot to turn the glass right-side-up, flooding the table and causing a river of white to flow onto the laps of two other students.

The teachers believed that the best way for blind people to cook was to combine the use of microwave ovens with some of the small, easy-to-handle electric grills that cooked food on both sides at the same time. Brenden worked on a grill plugged on television by heavyweight boxer George Foreman, and he was pleased to learn that he could easily cook foods such as chicken or fish.

The center also used specialized microwaves. Brenden discovered that the best voice processor was one made by the Hamilton Beach Company. The voice not only took you through all the various settings of the oven but also kept you aware of the time in one-minute increments. So now he could bake a potato with his chicken or fish.

As the days went by, he had to admit to a certain feeling of accomplishment in learning to perform these seemingly basic domestic tasks, but he still felt inept and disabled.

One of the women in his class had a husband and four children, and she had always loved to cook. She figured out a method for placing dots around the dial of a regular oven that would allow her to set the appropriate temperature and prepare her own Thanksgiving turkey. He didn't think he'd ever be doing that, but he did agree that her effort was impressive.

From the time Brenden was a little boy, he loved coffee. He didn't know why, but he just loved it, and as an adult, his day could not begin without it. He was happy to find that once again Hamilton Beach had made a coffeepot that allowed you to place your cup under a spout, activating the pouring process and eliminating a blind person's propensity for spilling.

There was also another voice-actuated device called a liquid indicator, shaped like a probe. When you placed it in a bowl, glass, or cup, it beeped as liquid was poured at one pitch and then beeped again in a higher tone when it reached the desired level.

There were a lot of fun toys, Brenden thought, but they were valuable only if you wanted to work hard and learn to use them. And he figured that he was only here to check them out for a little while; he wouldn't be around long enough for it ever to matter. The exception was computer technology, something Brenden had always been fond of, dating back to his love of video games.

He already owned a powerful laptop and was surprised at the sophisticated programs that were available on both Freedom Scientific's JAWS and HumanWare's Window-Eyes. As he typed, a voice told him exactly what he input, and there was a verbal spell checker available to make sure he got it right.

Along with this remarkable software, Freedom Scientific manufactured a terrific reader that allowed him to read anything by first scanning it and then reading it back in any one of over a hundred voices. He chose a guy named Perfect Paul, who sounded a lot like a good sports announcer, and the freedom to read a newspaper, magazine, or book was the only part of rehab that really brought a smile to his face.

Even more remarkable was the technology made by a company called Sendero Group. These amazing scientists created voice-actuated GPS units that could be either worn on the wrist or carried in the palm of your hand. And, exactly like the units found in anyone's automobile, this GPS technology made it possible for a blind person to know where he was at any given moment and program an accurate route.

In a weak moment, he told Charlie, "Some of this stuff is really pretty special. It's almost like being sighted." And then he added, "Almost."

EVEN THOUGH THE SCIENCE WAS truly remarkable, Brenden was still blind, and he knew life would never be the same. Science could not overcome the despondency of a young man broken in spirit and angry at his circumstances.

Lying in bed night after night, unable to sleep, Brenden lived in the memories of what once had been. He could still picture the touchdown passes he had thrown to Charlie and the home runs he had hit out of the park in Little League. He tried to re-create the feeling of skiing downhill in Colorado powder, the snow flying up over his shoulders, and the speed taking him right to the edge of danger. And then there were the memories of climbing, climbing high above the timberline with the sun so remarkably bright against the clearest of blue skies. He remembered his feeling of high accomplishment when he received his diploma at medical school and began the work he had dreamed of all his life. Worst of all, he pictured Lindsey's face and cried into his pillow, knowing he would never see it again.

No matter what guys like Barnes said or how many parlor trick skills he learned in rehab, the reality was that the man who had been Brenden McCarthy was gone, now replaced by a blind man who felt sorry for himself and lacked the will to go on.

He railed at God for cheating him of his sight. What had he done to earn this punishment? Who had he hurt so badly that he now had to live with this curse? Was there some mystery he was to understand and accept?

None of it made any sense to him, and though he grudgingly admitted that some of what he was learning was interesting, he had no hope that his future could ever be as meaningful as it would have been had his vision remained 20/20.

After a particularly difficult day in class, he came home to spend the weekend with his mother and Gus. It was the week of Halloween, and the air had taken on the first cold signature of winter. Brenden shivered in his light windbreaker as he tapped his way across the patio to the back door.

Before he could get there, Gus whizzed around the corner and dropped a tennis ball at his feet. Brenden bent to pick it up, but it rolled away, forcing the dog to grab it and try again. The second time, Brenden still couldn't find it on the ground, so the next time, Gus decided that he had to place the object right in his young friend's hand.

"Atta boy, Gus," Brenden said. "We haven't done this for a while, have we, fella?"

Over the next twenty minutes, the ball game was wonderful. The little dog raced around the yard, chasing the ball until he was exhausted, and the man enjoyed doing something that he always loved to share with this great animal.

His mother watched all this from the window, crying and laughing at the same time. Something was changing—each trip home showed progress. It was almost as if Brenden was beginning to decide that life really had possibility.

At dinner, his mother noticed that Brenden was getting better at cutting his meat, and though he was not yet willing to try pouring milk, he was able to move around the house with the beginnings of—what? Freedom?

Over apple pie à la mode, Mora broached the subject on her mind. "Brenden, have you talked to anybody at rehab about the possibility of a dog? I mean a guide dog?"

Brenden cut her off. "Gus is enough for me, Mom. I don't want to be responsible for anyone else or anything else. I don't even know if I can ever make it on my own, let alone have to take care of some big animal."

"I don't think that's the point," his mother put in. "From everything I've read, the idea is that you and the dog will learn to take care of each other. Seems to me that if you're going to move out of here soon and live on your own, you're going to need help, and I know you hate using the cane. Wouldn't you just consider giving it a try? I've read online about the guide dog school in San Rafael, and frankly, I've already written for an application."

"Mom—"

"Brenden, just give it a try. Please. If you go there for a couple of weeks and it doesn't work, there's no harm done. You can always come home. But I know how much you love Gus, and, well, I think a working animal could really make a difference in your life."

Brenden could hear the desperate sincerity in his mother's voice and decided that for now it would be simpler to go along with her, even if only to give Lindsey the idea that he was working to be independent.

After a pause, he said, "Okay, Mom," surprised to discover he could actually hear her smile. "Fill out the forms. If they'll take me, I'll go there and check it out."

Later that night, lying in bed with Gus snuggled close, Brenden was wide-awake. He realized he had made a commitment that postponed his plan B, in the event that he lost Lindsey. Instead of a clean way out, he was complicating his life.

"I don't know why I'm doing this, Gus. You're the best friend I have. I sure don't need another one."

The little dog moved deeper under the covers, seeming to agree.

chapter eleven

Mora hadn't wasted any time. Before Brenden could reconsider, his application was approved and his plane reservation made. He tried to understand why the idea of getting a guide dog didn't appeal to him. He loved animals. Gus was a case in point, and he certainly wanted to be independent. But as he lay in bed the night before he was to leave, he realized that somewhere in his mind he had not yet accepted the concept that he was blind. Did he think there was some marvelous medical breakthrough out there? A miracle, maybe, that would give him back his sight? He and his mother spoke to a number of famous ophthalmologists around the country to get other opinions, and all of the doctors agreed. He was permanently blind. That was his reality. That was the way it was.

The next morning, even with Lindsey's arms wrapped tightly around him and the warmth of her good-bye kiss still fresh on his lips, Brenden still wondered why he was headed for San Rafael, California, and Guide Dogs for the Blind.

The only thing he was sure of, as the girl kissed him again, arousing the passion that always burned inside him whenever she was close, was that his motivation—his complete motivation—was to hold on to Lindsey's love, no matter what it took. He didn't have a lot of faith in this journey, but right now he didn't have a lot of faith in anything, and if it all went bust, there was always . . .

How had he let his mother talk him into this ridiculous idea? He was blind, wasn't he? That was all that really mattered, and no dog was ever going to make the difference. All of the things he enjoyed in life, the outdoor activities and his hopes for medical practice, were taken away. So why was he on his way to San Rafael?

Lindsey turned him over to a United Airlines passenger service person, who would escort him onto the plane. He held the stick awkwardly in his right hand. *The cane*, he thought. *The symbol that told the world everything they needed to know about him. Brenden McCarthy. Blind.*

Now he was being patronized.

"Are we ready to go?" The voice of the airline woman asked, as if she were taking care of a little child.

Brenden stifled his anger and just nodded. Then there was the awkward dance between them as the woman tried to take his arm, and he tried to use the human guide system he learned during rehab. Eventually after jockeying for position, Brenden had the woman's elbow and followed her as she walked carefully down the Jetway. He had not been this careful when he climbed mountains, he remembered. Maybe he should have been.

Entering the plane, the overly solicitous woman was joined by a male steward, who almost tried to carry Brenden to his seat and wouldn't leave until he was sure the very physically fit young man was safely belted in.

"My name is Edward," he told Brenden. "Please call me for anything you need. Let me show you where your call button is."

Again, an awkward sort of dance occurred as the men clasped hands.

Now Brenden's seatmates began to arrive, adding to his already mounting frustration. The luck of the draw gave him two children—a squirmy baby on his mother's lap and a precocious kid of about four, who immediately began demanding things and kicking the seat when he didn't get exactly what he wanted when he wanted it.

It didn't take long for the boy to notice Brenden.

"What's that?" he asked with no preamble.

Brenden didn't respond.

"What's that stick?" he asked again, insisting by his tone that Brenden answer him.

"It's called a cane."

"What's it for?" the kid asked.

"To beat little children," Brenden said, regretting the words as soon as they were out of his mouth.

"That's not very nice," the mother said, coming to the defense of her child.

"I know." Brenden shrugged. "I'm very sorry. I've only been

blind for a little while. I kind of hate it, if you know what I mean."

"Okay, Tommy. Now, leave the man alone," the mother said.

After settling her children down, the woman couldn't help her curiosity. "How did it happen?" she asked, the pity obvious in her voice.

"I fell," was all he said, not willing to tell his story to a stranger. He was grateful to be able to put on his Bose headphones and cut off any further conversation.

So now, listening to Eric Clapton as the plane took off, he took slow, deep breaths, trying to relax and consider what he knew about the guide dog program and the days ahead. Very little, he realized. The truth was, his mother had filled out his application, and she was the one pushing him to do this. Why would he want a dog? Frankly, why would he deserve one? Or anything or anyone else, for that matter. No one really wanted him, except his mother, and he believed a lot of that was some form of maternal commitment.

He had no value, no cachet in the world. And now he was going to become the master of a big dog? *I don't think so*, he thought. *I really don't think so.*

And yet, something put him on this airplane. Something made him sit in this seat and endure the humiliating questions of a kid and his mother. Something sent him to the guide dog school. Was it hope for independence? Was the need to be a part of the world still basic to who he was as a person? Was it to retain—or win—Lindsey's love?

Lindsey, Lindsey, Lindsey.

At that point Clapton sang some piece of blues about a woman doing some guy wrong. In a moment of stark candor, the thought hit him that this could be what he would soon face with Lindsey. No, he couldn't believe it. She truly loved him, didn't she? And if she did, his blindness wouldn't matter. Love sticks it out through the tough stuff. But on the other hand, why should a beautiful, gifted girl like Lindsey hitch her wagon to a blind horse? He would hold her back, and she was too spirited to be held back. It didn't make sense for her to stick with him, and if she chose to call it quits, he couldn't blame her.

No! Brenden thought with a passion that made him grit his teeth. *I can't let it happen. I will not hold her back. I will show her that I can become a whole person. And if I can't, well, I still have my other option.*

After touching down in San Jose, a retired schoolteacher with a lifetime of wisdom met Brenden. He introduced himself simply as John, and as Brenden quickly learned, a blind father had raised him with a no-nonsense philosophy that said anything was possible if you were willing to work hard. This guy could care less if Brenden was blind or had two heads. He was what used to be called in the vernacular a man's man. He figured that everybody was the same until proven different. And so, for the first time since his accident, Brenden found himself relaxing and sharing normal conversation with this guy on the one-hour drive to the school.

"What's it like there, John? I mean, what does it look like?" Brenden asked.

"Oh man," John said, "it's beautiful. The country is really

rolling and lush. The buildings are Spanish California–type architecture with a whole lot of brick and tile. The kennels, well, the kennels are nicer than most of the hotels you find in this country. And the dorms, all the students get their own rooms, along with three squares prepared by some really good cooks. All in all, it's a good life while you're there. You'll be with us for a month, right? Because it's your first dog?"

"I guess so," Brenden said.

"Oh, they've done the job with people tougher than you." John laughed. "Some of the war vets we've had in here are really hard cases. You're a picnic compared to those guys. Do you know that since we opened this campus in 1956, we've put over ten thousand teams into the field?"

"Teams?" Brenden asked.

"Yeah, my friend, that's what you're going to be—a team, you and the dog."

Brenden didn't answer, and John didn't push him. They drove in silence until they reached the campus and went through the gates. Brenden was struck by the myriad smells, and John noticed him sniffing the air.

"You like the smells, Brenden? I do too. All the plants were chosen to make all you new students understand how glad we are to have you here. Let me help you with your bags and introduce you to the admissions staff."

John took Brenden to his room and allowed him to unpack.

"You're just in time for dinner," John told him. "Now you'll find out what I meant when I said the food was great."

John escorted him to the dining room and seated him at a

round table with what felt to Brenden like six or seven other students.

The housemistress introduced him. "Everybody, this is Brenden McCarthy. He is here for the first time, so don't scare him away with your horror stories."

There was laughter around the table.

A voice at the other end put in, "First time? Wow, I got my first pooch in the 1960s, and now I'm back for my fifth."

"Heaven help the dog, Jimmy," a woman's voice put in. "You're such an old curmudgeon, any animal you get is going to be in a hurry to get back to the kennel."

"Oh, you're just jealous, Lorraine"—Jimmy laughed, apparently knowing exactly who she was—"because the last time we were here, I got Leah, the most beautiful golden retriever in the history of the world, and you got the boxer—Leonard, wasn't it? Remember? That's when they were training boxers—the great slobberers of the world."

The woman laughed, taking it well. "Yeah, but he was a great old boy, my Leonard, a great old boy."

"So, Brenden, what do you want?" Jimmy asked. "They've got goldens, black Labs, yellow Labs, a few shepherds, and then this new breed, the Labradoodle. That's a combination Lab and poodle. I've heard they're really smart, but what do I know? I'm blind."

Laughter again rang out around the table. Brenden found himself wondering how they could all be so cavalier about their disability. Hadn't some of them lost their sight along the way because of an accident, just like him?

Jimmy asked again, "So what do you want, pal?"

"I don't know," Brenden said tentatively. "I guess I'll just take whatever they give me."

"Well," Jimmy said, "you're in Harold Smith's class—Smitty, we call him. That means you'll get a great dog no matter what it is. Smitty's the best. The only problem is he likes dogs more than he likes people."

Lorraine jumped in again. "That's not true, Jimmy. He just likes dogs more than he likes an old pain-in-the-rear like you." This time the laughter was even louder.

Brenden realized that most of these people had been down this road before and were both extremely excited and comfortable. He couldn't understand it. He was here largely because his mother had pressured him and because he knew without a doubt that if he didn't regain his independence, he wouldn't be worth anything to Lindsey. He understood perfectly that he had to become her equal in all things or their love would die. All this optimism about dogs was just too much.

Just then, a sliding glass door at the far end of the room opened, and Brenden heard someone stride in with confident steps. Enthusiastic applause broke out. Smitty had arrived.

"Good evening, ladies and gentlemen," he announced. "Welcome to Guide Dogs. You have the distinct honor and pleasure of being members of my class."

A smattering of good-natured booing followed this comment.

"Oh, you people are just sorry you're not bald and handsome like I am." Smitty laughed. "That's right, ladies, handsome and bald and getting older."

"Not as old as me," Jimmy piped in.

"No, Jimmy, that's true. No one is as old as you."

Again, laughter.

"All right, everyone. You know the rules, but if you're new and you've read your material, you've learned that your dogs will not be presented for the first three days. You'll be working Juno."

Jimmy groaned. "That means me too, Smitty?"

"Yes, it does, Jimmy. Your technique has probably become too sloppy over the years. You're likely taking too many shortcuts. It's about time we straightened you out."

Brenden didn't know exactly what Juno was, but he had heard that it related somehow to simulating what the dogs did with their instructor.

"It's going to be a long day tomorrow," Smitty went on, "with a lot of walking. Breakfast is promptly at seven. The work begins at eight. We'll start with a general lecture on the work and then go out into the beautiful streets of San Rafael to begin our training. Take some time and get to know each other. Some of you already know where your rooms are, but we'll be around to help any of you who aren't sure. Just let us know whenever you're ready to go to bed."

After more applause, Brenden noticed that most of the students immediately fell into excited conversations. They were extremely enthusiastic about meeting the dogs, while all Brenden wanted to do was go home.

Smitty watched all this, observing the young man sinking further and further into himself. He thought about McCarthy's application, how it spoke of his love of sports and outdoor activities, of his graduation from medical school and his desire to live in downtown Denver. Smitty had actually been thinking about Nelson for this young man, but now as he watched him, he wasn't sure. Maybe Nelson would have to wait for the next class; that is, if nobody caught on to his deception.

He crossed the room and introduced himself. "I'm Harold Smith," he said. "You're Brenden McCarthy, right?"

The handshake told Brenden that this guy had worked hard throughout his life. His hand was gnarled and strong, but there was also friendship and warmth in the shake. Brenden had noticed over the months since he lost his sight that he could learn a lot from a handshake, and it was clear to him that this one said, "Glad to meet you. I hope I can help." Right now, Brenden didn't want any help. He wanted to go to bed.

"Excuse me," he said, without engaging in conversation. "Could you show me my room, please? I think I'd like to call it a night."

"Oh sure," Smitty said. "Take my arm. Right this way."

They moved down the corridor, and Smitty refamiliarized Brenden with his bedroom and bath.

"Well, good night," Brenden said, sitting down on his bed.

"Listen, McCarthy," Smitty said, sensing the young man's disconnect, "I want you to know I'm here for you; I mean, any extra attention you need, any special work with the dog that we'll pick for you. I know from your application that you had a tough break with your accident, and I'm sure it's not easy to begin living as a blind person. But if you're willing to try, these incredible animals can make a big difference in your life."

Brenden didn't even nod, and Smitty was forced to go on. "Like I said, we'll begin tomorrow morning after breakfast, and actually I'll be working with you for the first couple of days. I very much look forward to sharing a partnership, so get a good night's sleep, okay?"

Again, Brenden sat mute, and Smitty quietly closed the door.

For a long time after the trainer left, Brenden just sat on his bed, not moving, deep in thought. He hated his circumstance. He hated the idea that he was thought of as one of these people. They were blind, handicapped, disabled, and yet they seemed happy in their pathetic state. Didn't they know what the world was really like? How much they had lost or would never understand? The changing of the seasons? A rainbow? A beautiful smile? They were blind.

And then it hit him like a crippling blow in the stomach. So was he: Brenden McCarthy, doctor, mountain climber, fiancé to Lindsey. He was just like them. No better, no worse. He was blind. And tomorrow he would begin to learn to use a dog, an unmistakable symbol of his disability.

He put his head in his hands, overcome by the emotion of the moment, overcome as his reality enveloped him. Not for the first time, the tears began to flow. The sobs were gut-wrenching, and they came from a place of utter desolation. There was no catharsis in his crying, no easing of the pain, no opening of the doors to therapeutic understanding. Brenden was bereft of self-worth, a shattered spirit broken in heart, soul, mind, and body.

Eventually, when the crying subsided, he rolled onto his bed and mercifully slept, still in his clothes.

chapter twelve

At breakfast the next morning, Brenden felt the buzz in the room. He sensed the excitement all the students were feeling as they began the process toward relationships with new dogs and the independence that meant.

Their enthusiasm annoyed Brenden. Didn't they know? Didn't they understand that their dogs would brand them as—the word *handicapped* caught in his throat. Just the thought of it was almost impossible for him to take.

Smitty came in just as everyone finished breakfast. "Okay, boys and girls," he said, "your chariot is outside. We'll drive to the student lounge and pair you up with your instructors. Everybody have good walking shoes on? Wonderful. Because you're going to need them. By the time you're finished, your feet will be telling you you've covered a lot of miles. So let's go."

Everyone was loaded onto a bus, and when they arrived

the staging lounge—a school-owned building where people could take breaks and have soft drinks—Smitty was as good as his word. He put his hand on Brenden's shoulder.

"Are you ready to begin?" he asked.

The young man just nodded.

"Oh dear," Smitty said, "you're probably a night person—one of those guys who just doesn't like the morning. That's too bad." The trainer placed a leash and harness in Brenden's hands. "Here's your equipment—the second most important link to your dog and independence."

Despite himself, Brenden was curious. "The second most important link?" he queried.

"That's right. The most important one is love—the love the animal will feel for you and the love you'll feel for him. Trust goes along with that, but you can gain trust only if the love between you is so deep nothing can destroy it. You see, Brenden, the dogs are pure. Oh sure, they make mistakes, and sometimes they can behave in annoying ways, but it's never because they're being malicious or trying to hurt you, or even trying to gain an upper hand in the work. They're dogs—perfect in the way they ove us, imperfect sometimes in the way they behave."

"You sound as if you like the dogs more than you like peo-le," Brenden suggested.

Smitty laughed. "You got that right, bud. People disappoint u, but dogs never do. Come over here."

Smitty led Brenden to an area of the lounge along a wall and his hands on—what? "What is this?" Brenden asked.

"What do you think it is?" Smitty said.

"It's—it's—it's a make-believe dog?"

"You got it, and what I want you to do is practice putting on the harness and leash. Feel how it fits. The harness slides right over his head and then buckles around his chest. The leash attaches right there to the choke chain on his neck. Go ahead. Try it."

Once Brenden buckled the harness in place, Smitty went on.

"Now, check out the handle of your harness. That's your rudder. That's the way you're going to read every input, every nuance of your animal. The secret to guide work, along with establishing love and trust, is to be able to interpret each other, and Brenden, my boy, you'll be amazed at how much these animals understand. Frankly, they know much more than we ever give them credit for. They can feel when you're nervous or apprehensive. They can feel when you're happy or sad. They know whether you're having a good day or a bad one. And all of that will be reflected in the way they work for you.

"For today, I'm going to be your dog. We're going to take a walk, and I'm going to hold the end of the harness, keeping forward pressure so that you get the idea of interpreting my motion. Now, I admit it's not the same as working with a dog because I'm standing upright on two legs, and the dog is moving along on four, with the signals all coming from the way he moves and angles his shoulders. But after thirty years I've become pretty good at approximation. So let's take a walk."

They moved out of the building, Smitty exerting constant pressure on the harness, with Brenden tentatively following.

"I can feel you're a little nervous, Brenden," Smitty said. "If

I can get that feeling from the harness, you can bet the dog will know right away, so don't be afraid. Step right out. Neither the dog nor I will ever let anything happen to you."

Smitty came to a stop at the corner. "Okay," he said, "let's talk about the environment you're going to be working in. We are very fortunate here in San Rafael because the lettered streets A through E run east and west, and the numbered streets one through five run north and south. So it's easy for us to design routes for you to train on. Over the next few weeks, you'll hear me say things like, 'Go to Third and B.' What would that mean to you?"

"Well, I suppose it would mean I'd walk three blocks east, cross to the left or south, and then walk four blocks."

"Well," Smitty said, allowing a smile, "I got a smart one. That's right, Brenden. It's very important as you adjust to your dog and your blindness that you learn to picture the environments in which you work. The dog will remember a lot, but an animal is only as good as the capacity of his master to have a picture in his head. Do you get it?"

Brenden nodded.

Smitty went on. "That's an advantage you have over somebody who has always been blind. Now let's practice walking up to a curb. The dogs are trained to move forward smartly, keeping pressure on the harness until they come right up to the edge. Then they're to stop with your lead foot lined up so that your toes are square to the line we're going to walk when we step off to cross. Do you understand?"

"I think so," Brenden said, not really getting it.

Smitty could see the obvious puzzlement on the young man's face. "Don't worry about it," he said. "Let's just try one. The curb is about twenty yards from here in a straight line, so let's walk up to it. Here we go. Give me the command forward."

"What should I call you?" Brenden asked. "Should I just say, 'Forward, dog'?"

"No. Use my name, and give the name first. Say, 'Smitty, forward.'"

Brenden laughed. "This is great. I'm finally in control."

"That's exactly right," Smitty said, touching Brenden's shoulder. "That's exactly what we want. By the end of this month, we want you to be able to control your dog because the dog wants to work for you. Now give me the command."

Brenden took the handle of the harness. "Smitty, forward."

The man stepped out at a brisk pace, snapping the harness with aggressive forward pressure. Brenden was forced to keep up. As they reached the curb, Smitty stopped abruptly enough that Brenden stepped over the edge. Smitty's free hand flashed out, protecting the blind man from falling.

"You see," he said. "I told you. The dog will come up to the edge of that curb smartly. You have to be alert. Let's try it again."

The next time Brenden stopped perfectly with his toes square to the line of the crossing.

"Okay," Smitty said. "Now give me the command again."

"Smitty, forward," Brenden said. But as they crossed, the trainer purposely slowed. Brenden was not feeling pressure in the harness.

"Encourage me," Smitty said. "Encourage me to pick up the

pace. Sometimes dogs are afraid when they make a crossing with a new person. Tell me to hop up—that's the command they all know—and use my name. Come on, Brenden, encourage me."

Brenden laughed. "Okay. Hop up, Smitty, let's go, boy. Come on. Hop up."

"Remember, name first."

"Smitty, hop up."

The trainer picked up the pace and arrived, stepping up the curb an instant before Brenden did and stopping.

"Brenden, the dogs are trained to put their front feet on the curb to let you know that you're going to be stepping up. After a while, they won't do that—I mean, when you go out into the world. You'll just make the crossing, and the dog will learn to just give you a feel for pause as they step up. That's part of the nuance that we talked about: the seasoning, when the dog begins to read you as much as you read him."

As they walked along the next block, Smitty talked to Brenden about the different kinds of curbs he would encounter.

"Not all curbs are straight. You may remember from the time you were sighted. Sometimes curbs are rounded. Those are much harder to grasp for the student, and you have to trust your dog to line you up squarely to the direction you want to go. Then, there are the wheelchair ramp curbs. Those can be really tricky because the dogs tend to stop early at the top of the ramp rather than taking you all the way to the edge of the curb. There's also what we call flush curbs. You encounter these in a parking garage or an alley, and the break is not really a curb. It's just sort of a space in the street. The dogs understand these things, but very often masters force the animal over the edge, and sometimes the dogs start to take these kinds of crossings for granted. You'll really have to use your ears and be aware of what you're doing, most particularly listening to traffic. This work takes concentration, Brenden, a lot of concentration, but the rewards are worth every bit of effort you'll put into becoming a good team."

Brenden couldn't help but be touched by Smitty's enthusiasm, and that glimpse of hope that he felt on the way to the guide dog school once again made a fleeting appearance.

"Okay," Smitty went on, "when we get to this curb and I stop, we're going to make a lateral crossing. To do that, I want you to give me the command, 'Smitty, around,' and then step back and allow me to move up to the curb on your left. Do you understand?"

"Yes, I get it, Smitty," Brenden said.

"Okay, here comes the curb."

Brenden stopped perfectly and gave the trainer the command for around, lining up for the north/south crossing. The pair did it very well.

"Nice job, Brenden," Smitty said. "You have potential."

Over the next three hours, the pair worked on walking through the door of a building, finding an elevator, and searching out an empty chair in a crowded restaurant. After the lunch break, Smitty talked about how to correct a dog when the animal makes a mistake.

He did this with a vivid demonstration. He and Brenden came up to a curb, and Smitty stepped right out without pausing, causing Brenden to trip slightly.

"Drop the harness," he said, "and take the leash in both hands. Now, jerk the choke chain until it tightens as you tell the animal no."

Brenden practiced this three or four times, once using the phrase *bad dog* along with the word *no*.

"Don't ever say that," Smitty said. "The dogs are never bad. They are just wrong. You never want to do anything to break the animal's sense of self-worth. It's critical that they feel as good about themselves as you feel about your success as their working partner."

Brenden was surprised at how much there was to learn, and reluctantly he had to admit to himself that he actually enjoyed the experience. He couldn't help but appreciate Smitty's ability, and he found that he really liked the guy's company. Smitty was a teacher, and Brenden always respected those who knew more about things than he did.

In the afternoon the work was repeated, but this time Brenden was introduced to the simulator. This four-wheeled contraption, designed in Denmark, allowed the men to attach the harness to the vehicle, and the trainer walked behind, creating momentum by pushing the odd-looking contraption forward. This was important, because now the student had open space in front of him without the instructor there as a buffer.

By the end of the second day of class, Brenden and Smitty had covered virtually all of San Rafael's downtown area, and even an athlete like Brenden had to admit he did have sore feet. He couldn't believe Jimmy, the old guy. His enthusiasm was catching as he held court during dinner the second evening.

"Okay, everybody," he said, the passion obvious in his delivery. "One more day of this Juno crap, and we will meet our dogs. Tomorrow night, boys and girls, we get to know man's best friend."

"You mean your only friend, don't ya, Jimmy?" Lorraine never let up on him.

The old man led the laughter. "You're just upset, Lorraine, because we didn't fall in love years ago. Maybe it's not too late."

Brenden heard something whizz through the air—did Lorraine actually throw a roll? Judging from the soft thud and Jimmy's laughter, Lorraine had apparently hit her target.

"I don't think you're blind, Lorraine," Jimmy said. "That's much too fine a shot. Maybe I should have fallen in love with you. That probably would have been the best thing that ever happened to you."

Lorraine sighed. "Oh brother." But there was a smile in her voice, and everyone at the table, including Brenden, could feel it.

After dinner, students were separated out to have one-on-one interviews with their trainers. The class of twelve was divided into four groups of three, with four instructors assigned, and as the evening went on, gradually trainers invited students to join them in a quiet room for a one-on-one talk.

Actually, all of the instructors evaluated the students over the course of the first couple of days. But now it was time to try and put the pieces together, allowing trainers to create the people/animal matches that would lead to wonderful life fulfillment for both.

Smitty talked through a few details on Brenden's application.

"Well, Brenden, I see from your application that you're very much an outdoorsman and that you love sports. Did you play many sports in high school and college?"

"Yeah," Brenden said, his face taking on a dark expression. "Yeah, I played everything—quarterback on the football team, captain of the baseball team, point guard on the basketball team. And then there was skiing and hiking. Most particularly"—he paused—"most particularly, mountain climbing."

Smitty jumped in, understanding. "That's where you got hurt, wasn't it, Brenden?"

"That's how I went blind, you mean," Brenden said.

"Okay," Smitty said, "that's how you went blind. So?"

"So, everything," Brenden said. "That's how I became"—this time, the words poured out—"that's how I became handicapped, or—what do they like to call it now?—disabled or challenged?"

"But that's not why you're here," Smitty said. "You're here to gain the independence, or maybe I should say the interdependence, that comes when you fall in love and share your life with a friend—a furry one, for sure, but you'll never have a better, more loving pal. And by the way, dogs are the ultimate chick magnet. The women flock to a good-looking dog. You'll never be short on dates. Do you have a girl?"

"I had one," Brenden said quietly. "I don't know anymore."

"Well," Smitty put in immediately, "when you bring a pooch home, she's going to love you both. The fastest way to a girl's heart is to hook her up with a Lab, a golden, or a shepherd. Wait and see."

Brenden found himself getting a little fed up with this whole sanctimonious idea that if you had a dog everything would be just peachy-keen.

"Listen," he said, "you make it seem as if the dogs make everything just hunky-dory. I mean, if you have a dog, life is perfect."

"I didn't say that," Smitty said. "Remember when we were working today and you tripped over curbs, and a couple of times I let you thump into bushes, and then there was the door that nearly hit you in the head. There will be a lot of that when you get your dog, because even though we've poured our hearts and souls into these animals, they are as new at this work as you are, and each of you will have to decide to invest in the other. That's what all of this is about, Brenden, a mutual investment in each other."

Both men were quiet.

"I don't know if I want all that," Brenden finally said. "I don't know if I want the responsibility, and I don't know if I really want to try that hard to be good at this."

"Well," Smitty said, not hiding the sarcasm, "what's the alternative? A cane? You already told me you hated the stick. Or just hanging out in your house, letting your mother take care of you?"

"Shut up," Brenden said. "That's not fair. I've only been blind a little while."

Smitty softened. "I know that, Brenden. I really do know that, but I swear, if you give the dog and me a chance, we'll give you the greatest gift in the world."

"What's that?" Brenden asked, leaning forward in his chair, interested in the answer.

"Freedom," Smitty said. "Wonderful, blessed freedom."

Brenden thought about that as he lay in his bed later that night. He thought about how much he really wanted freedom, how much he really wanted to feel alive. Again, there was that faint glimmer of hope, like a butterfly flitting around in his stomach. Was the trainer right? Could he love an animal? Was freedom possible?

AT ABOUT THE SAME TIME, Smitty also lay awake, thinking his own thoughts. Was this the guy he wanted for Nelson? Had he found the person who could make it happen with the energetic black Lab? It would be risky, he considered. What if Brenden cracked, folding up like a cheap suit at the animal's intensity? What if he went home, beaten, and Nelson was forced to return to the kennel one more time? Could the dog handle defeat? How many times could he think he had found the right master and then experience rejection without being shattered?

Smitty knew that animals have delicate psyches, just as people do, and he understood completely that Nelson had just about come to the end of his capacity for failed experiments. The next two weeks would tell him a lot, and he found himself tossing and turning, unable to sleep as he considered what would happen when the man and the dog began their odyssey tomorrow evening.

chapter thirteen

Dinner was over, and the moment had arrived. All the students moved into the big common room and sat in chairs spread out with enough space so that their animals could lie comfortably next to them.

Brenden sensed a change in the atmosphere. People were quietly anticipating what was to come. It was much like the feeling he used to get before taking the field for a big football game. Nervous anticipation, he decided. People on edge. And what was he feeling? Despite himself there was a sense of—what was it? Anticipation? Curiosity? Dread? Hope? He couldn't tell.

He still did not quite believe that he really wanted a dog, but he had to admit that the last two days with this guy, Smitty, had been—well, it had been interesting. He had learned a lot, and he noticed that his senses were much more alive than they had been when he was sighted or in the rehabilitation program. He at least acknowledged to himself that he was willing to experiment, to meet this new animal, to check it out and see what happened.

The sliding door opened at the far end of the room, and he heard the sound of jingling chains and leashes. Spontaneous and enthusiastic applause broke out. The dogs were here, and so was Smitty.

"Good evening, ladies and gentlemen," he announced. "Your best friends have arrived, or at least I hope so. Remember the basic rule. At this point in your relationship, the dogs know more about the work than you do, so you're going to have to earn their love. Because of the way things operate around here, with most of you coming back for your second, third, or—"

"Fifth dog," Jimmy put in.

Smitty chuckled.

"Or fifth, Jimmy. I know most of you, and so I've got a pretty good idea of the matches we've made. Let's begin. In deference to your age, Jimmy, we'll start with you. Stand up and take two steps forward."

Jimmy's chair squeaked as the old man stepped out. An assistant came forward with Nan, and as Jimmy's hands stretched out and touched her, tears began to fill his eyes and pour down his face.

"Oh Smitty," he said shakily, "you old son of a gun. You found another golden. Oh my, another golden."

Jimmy was hugging the young dog now, and she licked his face.

"A match made in heaven, Jimmy," Smitty said. "Made in heaven."

Lorraine was next, and she was given one of the new Labradoodles that Smitty said would be great for her to work with on the west side of Manhattan.

Now Smitty stood in front of Brenden. "Well, Brenden, I know it's your first dog, and you're probably pretty nervous, but I want you to know that I think I picked you out a great one."

Smitty was glad that Brenden couldn't see his eyes, because behind them was his passionate hope that this young guy might just be right for Nelson.

He went on. "I know we talked about your application and your desire to be active, so we chose an animal that we think can be just as enthusiastic. Let me introduce you to your new black Lab guide dog, Nelson."

Brenden heard the jingling of a collar and the click of nails on the tile floor as someone brought this Nelson across the room. What was he supposed to do? Reach out and pat the animal or stand still? He didn't know, and more than that, he felt embarrassed and somewhat awkward among these people who seemed to be so comfortable in their relationships with new dogs.

"Come on, Brenden," Smitty said, "reach out and pat him. He's right in front of you."

Brenden moved his hand tentatively forward, and his motion seemed to unnerve the young dog. He turned his head and sort of stepped back.

"Come on, Nelson," the woman handler said, encouraging, "meet your new master."

"Maybe we should forget it," Brenden blurted out.

Smitty interrupted. "Maybe you ought to get right down there on your knees, pal, and give him a hug. That's what they want. They want to know you love them."

Smitty didn't miss the way Brenden knelt in front of the dog. Thirty years of working as a trainer told him immediately that this newly blind guy still wasn't sure if he wanted an animal or not, and Smitty noted that he would have to continue to watch closely for all of the danger signs. Smitty hoped he hadn't made another mistake.

Brenden's hands were finally exploring the animal, feeling the contours of a large head, thick neck, broad shoulders, deep chest, short, coarse coat, and a tail that now wagged with delight at being petted, even if the touch was tentative.

"All he wants is to work and be loved," Smitty said. "Not too different from any of us, if you think about it. Now Andrea will give you his leash. Just tell him 'down,' and keep him right next to your chair while we give out the other dogs."

Over the next half hour Brenden listened to the overwhelming happiness as the rest of the class met their new guide dog companions. What he felt was a mixture of discomfort and fear as he realized how little he knew about working with animals.

Oh sure, he loved Gus. Gus was his friend. But their relationship didn't involve any direct responsibility, one for the other. He had to admit he was scared. Afraid of—what? Failure? He wasn't sure.

He held the leash tightly in both hands and never reached down to pat the animal that lay quietly on the floor next to his chair. Every once in a while the young man touched the dog with his foot just to make sure he hadn't moved, but he simply wasn't comfortable enough to make real physical contact.

He noticed that every time Smitty came by, the dog's tail thumped the floor. *That's who he loves*, Brenden thought. *He loves his trainer. Well, he probably doesn't have to worry. I may not be around long anyway.*

Smitty addressed the group again. "Okay everybody, you know the rules. No cheating and trying to work with your animal until we start class tomorrow. Just love them and keep them at heel, and don't let them mess with the other dogs. Let's have a nice social hour, and then we'll turn in. There'll be a lot of work tomorrow, so try to catch some real Zs, even though I know you'll probably be up all night checking to make sure that your new friend is real."

Jimmy interrupted again. "Hey, Smitty, is it all right, since I've had four dogs before this girl, if I teach her to go down the hall and find Lorraine's room?"

"Jimmy, you're impossible," Smitty said with a smile in his voice. "Okay. Breakfast is at seven. See you in the morning."

Smitty watched Brenden from a distance, understanding the tension the guy felt. *I'm going to have to get in this young man's head*, he realized, looking at him for probably the tenth time. *If I had it to do over again, I don't think I'd give Nelson to this guy. The dog is too good. As of now, I don't know if McCarthy can ever come to appreciate him, but I've been wrong before, so we'll try it. We'll see.*

When the social hour was over, Smitty made sure he accompanied Brenden and Nelson to their bedroom. The dog kept pulling on his leash, trying to get to Smitty. Brenden was surprised that the trainer completely ignored the animal.

"Why don't you talk to him?" Brenden asked. "He obviously wants to be with you and not me."

"That's true," Smitty said, "but you're his master now. Other than to correct him and work with you, I have to ignore him."

Brenden still didn't understand. "But isn't that hard?" he asked. "I mean to not pay attention to him?"

"It's the toughest part of what I do"—Smitty sighed—"when I have to give up a friend, but that's part of the job. There is compensation. When I see a team come together, it feels great. I hope that happens to you, McCarthy. Now reach down at the end of the bed. You'll find a tie down link, and I want you to attach Nelson's leash to it. Do you feel it?"

Brenden bent down and found what Smitty was talking about.

"When you go to bed, he may do some crying as long as he thinks I'm still in the building, but don't pay any attention to him. Just tell him no, and if he keeps it up, give him one reassuring pat. No more than that. If you give him too much love, he'll think that crying at night is okay. There's a lot of psychology in this process, Brenden. There's an awful lot to learn."

As the door closed and Smitty left the room, the Lab began to whine. Brenden hated the sound.

"Okay, fur ball, okay," he said, "just shut up, will ya? I probably don't want to be here any more than you do, but for now we're stuck with each other, so let's try to get a little sleep, okay?"

The dog's answer was to whine again, forcing Brenden to climb out of bed and pat him.

"Listen, Nelson," he said in the dark, "you seem like a nice enough fella, and I'm sorry you drew me. Let's just try to get along, all right?"

The animal sniffed the man as if he was trying to decide where Brenden was really coming from. Then he rolled onto his side, exposing his belly, and the man tentatively rubbed it. The dog's sigh said he was resigned to the idea that he would be staying here tonight, and he soon fell asleep. He probably thought his present circumstance was at least better than the kennel. Brenden climbed back into bed and fell asleep as well.

BRENDEN DIDN'T NEED HIS ALARM clock to wake him up the next morning. The big dog licked his foot. Somehow in the night, the man extended it outside the sheets, and his toes were very much in the animal's reach. The dog gave a good morning lick to each one.

Other people were already up. Brenden could hear the sounds of dogs and humans moving up and down the corridor outside his door, and he soon joined them. He was surprised when everybody headed outside before sitting down to breakfast.

"It's time to park our dogs," Jimmy said. "This is when you find out if you really want one, when you have to clean up after them."

"What are you talking about?" Brenden said. "You mean we actually have to—"

"That's right," another student's voice chimed in. "You have to get right down there and pick it up."

"Actually," Smitty said, "there's a technique, but you won't be learning that today. We have a common area for parking. These guys are just giving you a hard time, Brenden."

"Parking?" Brenden said. "That sounds like a pretty good word for what happens."

"You'll find out how good it is," Jimmy told him. "That's a word you really want your dog to know."

Everybody talked about the dogs during breakfast, giving first impressions and sharing how special each already thought his or her new friend to be. They all expressed feelings except Brenden. At this point, he had no feelings about Nelson. They were just there together, not bonded.

All the students crowded into vans, and at a little after eight, they arrived at the lounge to begin the first day's interaction with their new working partners.

As Brenden would quickly learn, every day began with obedience. Those basic commands of *come*, *down*, *sit*, *stay*, and *heel* reminded the dog he now worked for a new master and gave the student the confidence to believe that he could handle his animal.

This work went on through the morning, and after lunch Brenden was surprised when Smitty told him that they were actually going to be harness training with their dogs right away. He hadn't realized it would happen that fast.

They stood outside the lounge on the corner of First Street, an area that Smitty said was a long block of just straight walking.

"Don't worry," he told Brenden, "all you're going to do is

walk up and down here, maybe a hundred and fifty yards, to get used to the feeling of a real animal pulling on the harness. Okay? I have to warn you, Nelson is a particularly strong dog. When you give him the command, 'Nelson, forward,' you're really going to get a response, so be ready to feel some real torque in the harness. The key to good work is not in how hard the dog pulls but in how steady the pull is. If it's steady, you can read it and understand the subtleties, and I can tell you from my work with Nelson, his pull is wonderful. Are you ready? Okay, give him the command, and then follow your dog."

The butterflies were back in his stomach as Brenden took a deep breath. *My maiden voyage*, he thought. *It'll probably be like the* Titanic.

"Okay," he said. "Nelson, forward."

The animal turned his head to look at Smitty, first questioning and then taking on an expression of profound sadness.

I know, boy, Smitty thought. *You've been through this twice before, but it has to work out this time, Nelson. It has to work with this guy.*

"Again, Brenden," Smitty said, determined. "Tell him forward again."

Brenden repeated the command. "Nelson, forward."

Again the big dog's eyes found his trainer, forcing Smitty to look away. Knowing what he had to do, the trainer reached out and gave the animal a sharp tap on the shoulder.

"Tell him again, Brenden," Smitty said. "This time be even firmer."

Brenden did as he was told. "Nelson, forward."

With one more look of resignation to his trainer, the dog moved out smartly, and for the first time Brenden felt the excitement of moving through space with the animal tracking in a perfectly straight line.

Smitty dropped back a few steps, and when he did, the dog's head turned to follow him, still hoping, even though he kept moving down the street.

"Brenden," Smitty told the new handler, "correct your dog and say, 'No, straight.'"

The big dog understood he had been corrected. He still wanted to work for Trainer. That's who he loved. But the man held the leash and the harness, and the animal had been conditioned to always obey the harness. Discipline took over. Nelson settled down and began to show Brenden why Smitty believed that this dog was the best he had ever trained.

Over the next hour they moved up and down the straight street, gaining confidence with every pass. For the first time, Brenden was in a good mood as they joined the others for dinner that evening. He actually engaged in conversation and found that some of the students were people he really enjoyed.

People, he thought. *These are real people. They're blind, but their hopes and dreams and feelings are just like everyone else's.* The conversations ranged from sports to politics, music to good books, but inevitably came back to the commonality of disability and dogs. Brenden was surprised to learn how many different jobs were represented in this class.

There was Alberto, a Puerto Rican American who lost his sight through retinitis pigmentosa and was now living in

Boston working as a computer programmer for a major software company.

Lorraine was a social worker, spending her life making a difference for senior citizens struggling to adjust to disability.

Jimmy had been a schoolteacher. "Imagine that," he told Brenden. "I taught public school for thirty-five years, most of it with a dog in the classroom. You think I was popular?"

Suzanne was a homemaker with three children. Eddie Harrison was a piano tuner who made his rounds using public transportation, taxis, and, most importantly, his dog to make a good living. There were a couple of musicians and a fascinating guy named Mark West, who was a trial attorney.

As Brenden listened, he wondered what he would do with his life. It was much too soon to know, but after the terrific day he'd just had with Nelson, he began to look at the possibilities with new eyes. *My life could be worthwhile*, he thought. Maybe he would find a reason to believe living could be worth it.

NELSON HAD BEEN THROUGH ALL of this before. In the beginning there had been a family with two little kids he loved to play with when he was a puppy. Then Smitty had been his master. He loved Smitty. Then he had been given to another man and after that to Man and Lady. He did the job, but he had been with none of them long enough to care about them. And now he took commands from this new guy, who smelled different from the others, who felt different when he held the harness, who commanded him differently and patted him differently.

The confusion and sadness showed in his eyes and in the way he always tried to search out Smitty whenever everyone was together. He couldn't understand. Why was he going through all this again? He was an unhappy black Lab, and what he wanted was to be with Smitty.

Another day ended with the man going to sleep and the big dog staying awake long into the night.

He knew it was wrong, but he decided to chew on the socks Brenden had left on the floor. His anxiety, along with his sense of frustration, made him restless and uneasy, and he just had to have something to bite on.

After the socks came the soft patent leather of Brenden's expensive loafers and then a flannel shirt that was one of the man's favorites. A warm breeze blew through the open window, and Nelson registered the sound of a car passing by on the main road just outside the campus. His animal brain connected *car* with *go*. *But where?* It registered. *To Smitty*. He needed to go to Smitty, and the need was impossible to fight. Placing his paws on the windowsill and looking out, he made a dog's uncanny assessment that if he jumped he could land on some bushes and then continue with a leap to the ground.

Okay, go! The screen crashed, and the big dog landed perfectly on the bushes and then on the ground. Shaking once, he trotted off—a black dog on a dark night in search of his master, in search of Smitty.

chapter fourteen

The crash of the screen jolted Brenden awake. Struggling to understand the sound, he remained still for a moment, waiting to see if some other kind of catastrophe would follow.

Soon he decided he was safe and remembered that he wasn't alone. "Hey, fur ball, are you okay?" he called.

There was no response anywhere in the room. Brenden tried again.

"Nelson. Come here, Nelson. Are you all right?"

Again there was no response, and Brenden climbed out of bed, not really worried but certainly curious. Not knowing his room very well and being newly blind, he moved slowly, his hands groping in front of him as he widened his circle. After finding no dog, his feet kicked—what was it? Reaching down, he was surprised to discover—what? The heel of . . .

"Oh no," he said out loud. "The heel of my shoe. My loafers."

Now crawling along the floor, it didn't take him long to discover the rest of the damage—his shirt, socks, and his shoes all chewed into pieces.

Feeling the air moving through his window and following the breeze, he came to the window, felt the broken frame of the screen, and figured it out. Nelson was gone, probably to Smitty, he reasoned.

"Well, good riddance," muttered Brenden, pitching the ruined shoe across the room. "I can't tell anybody about this until morning anyway, so I'm going back to bed. Good riddance, you destructive fur ball."

DAWN WAS BREAKING IN THE east, and Smitty was dreaming—something about Tahiti, swaying palms, and hula girls—when his sleep was disturbed by a sound that he recognized immediately. An animal scratched at his door, and not just scratching but demanding to be let in.

He stepped into his slippers, turned on the light, and crossed his living room and opened the door. He was almost knocked flat as Nelson burst in crying and yipping to express the joy, relief, and love that poured from his heart. He had found Smitty.

"Okay, Nelson, okay," the trainer said. "How did you get here, boy, and what kind of trouble are we in now?"

After giving the dog some water, Harold Smith showered and dressed, even though he didn't have to be up for another couple of hours. It was only thirty minutes later when the dog and trainer arrived at the school. None of the other trainers had shown up, and people were just beginning to stir as Smitty pulled his car into the parking lot and got out. He and Nelson went right to Brenden's room and knocked softly. When there was no response, he tried again more firmly.

"Go away," the voice said from inside, "and take Mr. Destruction with you."

"Come on, Brenden," Smitty said. "Open the door. Let me see if I can help."

"Go away," Brenden said again. "I'm not interested in you or your dog."

"Open up, man," Smitty said more forcefully, "or I'll get a master key. We have a responsibility to every student and animal to keep you safe, and I need to know what went on in there."

Slowly, the door opened, and Smitty saw the damage.

"Oh brother," he said. "You've really done it this time, Nelson."

The trainer crossed the room in three long strides, placing his hand on Brenden's shoulder. "First of all, pal—"

"Don't call me pal," Brenden interrupted. "We're not pals. We don't even know each other."

"All right," Smitty said, taking a deep breath while Nelson settled on the floor, not even considering that he had done anything wrong. "Okay, Mr. McCarthy, you should know that the school will replace anything that's damaged. It happens sometimes when our animals are going through withdrawal. The changeover isn't easy." Smitty couldn't help himself. "Especially when the dogs sense that the new person doesn't want them."

"Well, isn't he bright?" Brenden said sarcastically. "To figure that out?"

Smitty pulled on his memory. "Look, you told me that the reason you are here is to get back your independence. Is that right?"

Brenden considered and then answered grudgingly, "Yeah, that's right. I want to be independent."

"Then let me tell you something," Smitty said. "This dog can give that to you faster than any other method available. You've already experienced what it feels like when you're working together. I think you ought to give it a little time before you make any snap decisions. You know, the easy way out is just to feel sorry for yourself and figure that it's another bad break on the rocky road to living. If you want to get back to freedom and to normal life, this dog will give you the best chance."

Brenden sat quietly, thinking about what he'd just heard, thinking about Lindsey and independence.

"Okay," he said. "Okay. Let's see what happens, but get the screen fixed, and get me some money for the stuff your fur ball destroyed."

"Yes, sir, Mr. McCarthy," Smitty said, a touch of sarcasm in his own voice.

OVER THE NEXT THREE DAYS, Brenden and Nelson worked on curbs and turns. Nelson performed perfectly. The dog was matchless in his ability to move Brenden smartly up to a curb with the man's feet set squarely on the line that would take them across the street with accuracy and safety. When they reached the other side, Nelson consistently stopped with his front feet on the up curb until Brenden gave the signal to step up. Smitty explained that later, when they went out into the real world, it would be easy for Brenden to teach the animal not to stop, but just to pause on the up curb.

This actually happened on the second day because, unlike the other dogs, Nelson had already been out in the field. An instinct took over. Smitty couldn't help but be proud of the animal, and because Brenden was athletic he chose to let this particular discipline slide.

They also worked on left and right turns, with the young man learning to follow his dog closely. When it came to stairs, the dog had to learn not to move down the steps too quickly. It was important that the pace be steady, with the harness pressure not too extreme, which would cause the master to lose his balance. This was hard for all the dogs because it meant they had to maintain their own balance without resorting to sort of jumping down the steps.

Up to this point, all the trainers worked in close proximity to student and dog, sometimes moving a couple of steps ahead to encourage the animal's work, sometimes walking on the outside of the dog to help the animal maintain a straight line, and sometimes dropping back a few steps when the work was going well. In general, Nelson maintained the quality of his work without looking to Smitty for support.

Sunday came around at the end of the first week, and the students had a day off. Smitty was pleased to write in his training report that Nelson seemed to be accepting Brenden as a handler. The concern was that Brenden did not yet seem committed to accepting his new life with the animal.

"I hope," Smitty wrote, "that this will correct itself during week two. If it doesn't, I believe this candidate may not qualify as a graduate of the program."

Now the class moved into the next stage of training. During this period, the trainers introduced independent travel. Students and their dogs were trained to accomplish various outings around San Rafael.

First, in a planned environment, the team walked the same route a number of times, with the trainer expanding the distance at his discretion. The instructors encouraged independent travel, and they gave the new dog/person teams a set of destinations to reach on their own.

This was where the team had to begin to trust each other, and it was that element that worried Smitty very much when he considered the readiness of Nelson and McCarthy.

As he noted in the report, in the early stages they seemed to do okay because the route was simple. After leaving the lounge they would turn left on Fourth Street and follow it one block to D, where they would cross and make a right turn to the curb so that they would be, once again, facing Fourth Street.

When the traffic was clear, they'd cross and continue south to Third. Turning left, they would then walk down Third Street to C, and depending on how the team felt, they would continue two more blocks to A, where they would turn left, cross, and return to Fourth—basically walking a square grid.

Brenden had a distinct advantage over many of the other students because, though he didn't know it, he worked with a dog that had done this many times before. Like all the animals, Nelson's memory was photographic, and patterning was an element that all good guide dogs brought to the job.

Consequently, Brenden found himself feeling a sense of accomplishment during this elementary period of training. He also found himself having conversations with many of the other students about coping with blindness. He became interested as he learned that the group seemed to be divided when it came to the basic discussion of who had it tougher: people who were born blind and had grown up that way or those who lost their sight through illness or an accident.

He was sure that people like him must find it more difficult, but he was surprised when he found out that both groups believed they were the lucky ones. The people who had been born blind talked about how they had grown up learning to cope with the disability, while the people who had lost their sight in later years talked about how much it meant to have visual concepts in their heads.

Old Jimmy made a real impression on him when he said he hated the fact that over the years, he had lost his perception of some colors.

"I just can't remember purple," he told Brenden. "I can't pull in the picture anymore, and I don't remember my daughter's beautiful eyes. It's just been too many years. I can't keep the image in my head."

Brenden wondered if that's how it would be for him. How

long would he be able to remember the gold of the aspens in the fall? How long would he remember Lindsey's exquisite face and form? The idea of forgetting those glories made him sad and angry. And yet, something inside him—something fundamental to his character—made him remember old Jimmy and how much he had lost.

Casually, the young man dropped an arm over the old man's shoulders. "I'm sorry, Jimmy," he said. "I really am sorry. It's gotta be tough when you lose the colors, but think about how many people you've touched over the years. I mean, as a teacher and a husband and a father."

Jimmy smiled. "Now, don't go soft on me, kid. I figured you for a tough guy."

"Not that tough." Brenden shrugged. "Not that tough at all, Jimmy."

BY THE MIDDLE OF THE second week, Smitty allowed more and more space between Brenden, Nelson, and himself. He dropped back farther and farther when Brenden walked the route and hid in doorways to keep himself out of Nelson's sight line. No matter how hard he tried, however, the big black Lab always seemed to know where he was. He chuckled, remembering how keen the animal's senses were. *You just can't hide from a dog that wants to find you*, Smitty reminded himself.

Brenden had begun to freelance on the routes, being given the opportunity to enter stores, make purchases, and develop a sense of early independence.

All in all, Smitty thought, *things do seem to be going well. But I still feel there's something missing, and I think it's love.*

The route was one they had walked before. Certainly, they were in an area that Nelson knew very well. Smitty moved across the street to take up a position in the doorway of a hardware store. As he watched, he saw the problem coming at about the same time the big dog did.

Ahead was a new construction area that the team would have to pass, and the street was torn up to install new sewer lines. Men were working in hard hats with jackhammers, making it impossible to hear anything else. Smitty made one of those instinctive decisions based on his years of training. He decided to let the young man and the dog work out the problem. Frankly, he wasn't sure about Brenden, but he trusted the seasoning that Nelson had been given in the field, and predictably the dog made exactly the correct choice.

As he and Brenden moved closer to the sound, the animal slowed, maintaining harness pressure but easing his master away from the building to the outside of the sidewalk.

Smitty couldn't see exactly what was ahead of them, but Nelson did. A gaping hole in the concrete made it almost impossible to get through the area, and so the dog came to a stop, looking up at Brenden as if to say, "We need help."

Brenden felt cocky. Things had gone very well over the last few days, and he hated the sound of the jackhammers. Should he turn around and retrace his steps or try to carry out the assignment? He made an aggressive decision.

"Nelson, forward," he said. The dog didn't move. "Nelson,

forward," he commanded in a much firmer voice. Again the dog refused. There are moments in life when the human psyche is strung as tight as a bowstring—any vibration, any jarring, and the tension must be released.

Brenden snapped, breaking every rule of affection-based training. Brendan dropped the harness and used the leash with three violent pulls on the choking chain, causing the dog to drop to the ground.

Then in a voice full of anger, disgust, remorse, frustration, and sadness at the entire scope and tragedy of his blindness, Brenden roared at the dog, "Nelson, you miserable, useless animal, forward!"

The animal's eyes searched desperately for his trainer, and his whimper said, "I know I'm right. This is what I'm trained to do, what I'm supposed to do. I will not go forward."

Smitty arrived at that moment, grabbing Brenden by the shoulders and spinning him around.

"Give me the leash," he told Brenden, his anger filling the space between them. "You're done for the day, McCarthy, and maybe for good. You're an ungrateful jerk who's feeling sorry for himself and taking it out on the dog. That is not acceptable."

ARRIVING BACK AT SCHOOL, BRENDEN went to his room, and Smitty took Nelson to the kennels. After putting the dog away, he went to his office and sat down at his desk. The sun had set, and the light was fading.

Had he done the right thing—or had he overreacted and

been unprofessional? *I couldn't stand to see him break Nelson's spirit,* he thought. *I was right on the edge. I wanted to deck him.*

He pushed his chair back and swung around to look out at the darkening campus. Nelson had been right, of course, in refusing the command. Smitty realized, however, that he had just as much responsibility for Brenden's well-being as he did for the dog's.

What to do now?

Should he go to the director and say he thought this candidate was unfit to take an animal into the field, or should he try and talk to Brenden? There was so much potential there. Watching them together, he saw the possibilities for a tremendous partnership.

The trainer made a decision.

He crossed the courtyard to the dorms, where he checked the dining room and the social areas to see if Brenden was with the other students. Not finding him, he went to the young man's room and knocked. There was no answer. He knocked again, and again no one answered.

"Brenden," he said, "it's Harold Smith. Are you in there?"

This time the voice came from the other side of the door. "Leave me alone, Smitty. Go away."

Harold Smith took a deep breath. "What do you drink, McCarthy, when you're not here at school and you're out with your friends?" There was no response. "There's an English-Irish pub down at the end of the street, called The Old Head. I'd very much appreciate it if you would let me buy you a beer or whatever is your drink of choice. I think we could both use one."

After a short beat, Smitty heard the bed creak and Brenden's feet cross to the door. It opened. "Okay," he said, "you're probably right."

Fifteen minutes later they were sitting in a comfortable booth in a corner of the bar with two large steins of beer and a bowl of peanuts.

"Listen, bud," Smitty said, "I overreacted today, but you just can't treat a dog like that."

Brenden put down his beer. "I know that, Smitty," he said. "I've been thinking about it. I guess I'm just not cut out to have an animal. I'm not ready. There're still too many raw nerves, and I guess I just lose it sometimes."

"It's understandable, Brenden," Smitty said. "I can't imagine how difficult it is to adjust to being blind, especially when a guy is as energized as you are. But, Brenden," Smitty went on, leaning over the table, "this dog, this marvelous animal, represents your chance to be active again. Do you know why you have Nelson, why I picked him for you?"

Brenden was curious. "Why?"

"Because he's the best dog I ever trained, and because this is his last chance. He actually has been out in the field twice with two people who couldn't handle him. I matched him inappropriately. He has some quirks, like all aggressive animals do. I mean he likes to bite stuff sometimes, and there's never been food he doesn't want to eat, and he probably plays a little too rough. But, Brenden, he's brilliant and joyous and gutsy, and I have a feeling that's the kind of person you are."

"That's the way I used to be," Brenden said quietly. "I used to be that person."

"Brenden," Smitty implored, "you can be exactly that kind of person again. If you're just willing to hang in and work with your animal, there is nothing you can't do together. I know guys who jog with their dogs. There are people who take their friends swimming. Last year there was a woman who ran the Los Angeles Marathon with her golden retriever. I've trained people who live independently in New York City and others who work their dogs in rural country settings with no sidewalks. Brenden, these animals can be adapted to share life in any way you choose if you can learn to love your dog enough and believe in the bond that can grow to be as strong as any that you'll ever share with another human being."

The waitress brought another beer, and Smitty was still selling.

"Look, Brenden, what's the alternative? A life in the dark, living on the sidelines without ever getting in the game? I don't think that fits your personality, and I don't think you want the people you love to think of you that way. Didn't you tell me about a girl you really care for? What's her name?"

"Lindsey," Brenden said. "Lindsey Reynolds."

"Okay," Smitty said, "Lindsey Reynolds. The more you demonstrate the ability to take your place back in society, the more Lindsey will love you. Life is all about partnerships, Brenden, and in a partnership everyone has to pull his own weight. Nelson will make it possible for you to be equal in any life setting you choose, but it's all up to you."

Brenden took a big pull on his beer and sat back. "You really think I can do it, Smitty? You really think we can become a good team?"

"I do, Brenden," Smitty said, meaning it. "I believe you can become a great team, if you will commit to loving Nelson as much as I know he'll learn to love you. What do you think? Do you think we ought to get him out of jail?"

"Jail?" Brenden asked.

"He's back in the kennel, and he's not a happy black Lab."

Brenden laughed. "Okay, Smitty, let's break ol' Nelson out of prison."

Smitty smiled. It was a start.

THE TRAINER WAS RIGHT—NELSON was not a happy black Lab. He paced up and down the kennel like a tiger. Now and then he flopped down with his head forlornly between his paws, only to jump back up and resume his pacing. What did he do wrong? He knew Brenden was mad at him, and he was sorry for that because he really liked working with him. But Smitty—Smitty didn't take him home. He brought him here; he put down a dish of food and some water—but he didn't take him home.

The big dog raised his chin and howled—a cry so painful, so desperate, so lost that all the other dogs joined in, creating a cacophony of sound.

As the two men approached the kennel, Brenden heard Nelson's mournful voice. He was amazed at the sympathetic emotion welling up inside of him. In the animal's longing, he could feel his own aching for Lindsey, and this resonance between them made him want to reach out and hug the dog.

As they came to the gate, it was Brenden who first spoke to the animal in the dark.

"It's okay, Nelson. It's okay, boy. We're here. We're going to get you out of jail. Just a minute, pal. We'll get this gate open."

Smitty took the keys out of his pocket, and in a second the prison door swung open and Nelson was free. Something happened then, something Smitty would think about for a long time. Something he didn't expect.

Free to make his own choice, Nelson didn't come to the trainer. Instead, the dog ran straight to Brenden and literally tried to leap into his arms.

Smitty didn't understand it, and yet it supported the premise he had always believed: never underestimate the power of a dog's instinct or the love expressed by these remarkable animals. Nelson made a decision only the dog could fathom. Could it be some kind of apology for this afternoon's event, or could it be that he somehow sensed that Brenden needed him even more than the young man knew himself?

Smitty recognized that a corner had been turned. In Nelson's basic, primitive instinct, he chose Brenden as his alpha dog, his leader, his master.

Both men knew that something remarkable had just happened, and Brenden had to admit to himself that he was touched to his very core by the dog's honest expression.

All three looked forward to the next two weeks of work.

chapter fifteen

Everything was different now. Overnight, the dynamics between Brenden and Nelson took on a new aspect, and trust began to germinate as the central theme of the work. The dog was confident the man liked him, and the man began to feel an exciting sense of pride each time they enjoyed success. Even though their daily routes were getting more complicated, their flow and ability to read each other through the telegraph wire of the harness and leash made achieving their objectives a piece of cake.

When they entered a building, Nelson lined up the young man perfectly to find the door. All Brenden had to do was reach out with his right hand, follow the animal's nose, and—presto!—the door handle or knob was always right there.

Coming to a chair, Nelson placed his head right on the seat, making it easy for Brenden to sit, rather gracefully he thought.

And then there were escalators. It was in this part of the work that the feel between them became even more critical.

They were in a crowded shopping mall with escalators going up and down to the various floors. Smitty asked the team to move forward onto the little ramp that acted as a bridge from the ground surface to the moving stairs of the escalator.

As a newly blind person, this kind of surface change caused great trepidation in Brenden's psyche. He couldn't help being afraid, and Smitty saw it right away.

"Trust your dog, Brenden," he said. "Trust Nelson. Now remember, when he steps onto the escalator, drop the harness, use the leash, and feel the railing with your right hand. That's it. Keep one foot behind the other so that you're balanced on the stairs. Now move out smartly and don't be afraid. That's it. That's it. Trust your dog. Good job."

Smitty was right behind them as they all went up the escalator together.

"Okay, Brenden, remember, as we get off, give the dog plenty of freedom with his leash so that he can hop and not jam his feet in the rollers. Keep your right hand on the railing and just walk with him. That's it. Very good! Very good, Brenden."

By the third or fourth try the team was seamless in their efforts, and the young man again told his trainer that it was all just a piece of cake.

It was also during this week that the team was introduced to traffic checks, requiring the help of additional instructors driving vehicles. During these traffic checks, the master had to completely trust his dog, and Brenden was surprised to find that there were a few different kinds of checks. The simplest type was when the team stood at a crossing with the master telling the dog to go forward and the car either coming fast around a blind corner or jumping a light, forcing the animal to stop on a dime.

The second type of check occurred when the student would be halfway across the street when the light changed and cars began to move. The dog was forced either to hurry through the crossing or stop with cars whizzing close to the team.

The third and most complex of the traffic checks was the most difficult to deal with. This occurred when a vehicle pulled out of a driveway or parking garage before the blind person had a chance to hear it. The dogs had to be incredibly alert to handle these encounters, and Brenden was lavish in his praise of Nelson as the black dog led the class in accuracy.

At dinner that evening, old Jimmy told him, "You know, Brenden, I've had five dogs, and none of them worked as well as your Nelson. You got the best, boy, the best, and I hope you appreciate it."

Brenden really did appreciate the gift he had been given, and for the moment his life was on a positive upswing. He and Smitty were getting along, and he also had a number of conversations with his mother. He told her that being here wasn't really that bad and that his dog, Nelson, was tremendous. He also talked to Charlie, who told him that he intended to accompany Mora to Brenden's graduation.

The downer—the thing that caused his stomach to tighten up and his heart to skip a beat—was his lack of communication with Lindsey. Oh sure, they talked a few times during the three weeks, but he sensed a subtle but significant change in their relationship. It wasn't that she was cold or unfriendly or even disinterested in his progress. What was missing was—he struggled to get a handle on it—intimacy.

Their conversations just didn't sound like those of a young couple in love, and he found himself counting the days until he could be with her, willing them to go faster.

He cared a great deal about Nelson, but his real love was Lindsey, and she dominated the center of his thoughts.

But during the day Brenden was able to dismiss his concerns about Lindsey and focus on becoming a team with Nelson. When you're about to take a trip to San Francisco, ride the BART system, and practice as a team in the financial district, which included figuring out Embarcadero Square, learning how to get through revolving doors, and finding the front desk in crowded hotel lobbies, your mind better be in tune with your animal.

Revolving doors were challenging, Brenden learned, because you really had to have good technique to handle them. The dog was taught to walk up to the door, stopping with his nose just outside the spinning frame.

Smitty told Brenden to give the command, "Forward and around," and when he did, he was to drop the harness and let Nelson jump around to his right side, keeping his own body between the door and the dog.

The first time they tried it Brenden took a pretty good shot on the side of the head from the moving door, but he was able to shake it off, and by the third attempt they had mastered the technique.

Traveling by bus required the dogs to either lay in the aisle in the back of the vehicle, facing forward so that no one would step on them, or scramble to get under a seat, keeping their paws and heads out of the aisle. None of the animals liked this part of the job, but all of them had to learn to accept it; and Brenden was surprised at how well Nelson adapted to whatever circumstance challenged him.

In a phone call to his mother, he tried to explain his present feelings. "Mom, the bottom line is that I don't really know how I feel about myself, about what I'm going to do, who I'm going to be, or how I'm going to handle this new life. But I am amazed at what goes on here at the guide dog school. I mean, these dogs are incredible, and they're all about service. There is something so pure in the way they do their jobs. They care first and foremost about us. Even now, I'm a brand-new guy in this dog, Nelson's, life, and yet I can feel that in every minute of his work, he's trying to take care of me. When I first got here, I resented all this stuff, but now, well, now it actually feels pretty good."

"That's wonderful," Mora said. "I'm anxious to meet your Nelson when Charlie and I come out for graduation. Have you heard from Lindsey about whether she'll be able to join us? The offer still goes, you know. I'm happy to buy her a ticket."

There was a pause on the other end of the line, and Mora heard her son sigh. "Oh, she told me that she's just swamped with work right now. I—I understand. I'll see her when I get home."

Mora could hear the sadness in her boy's voice but chose not to press him for more information.

During the fourth week of training, the class added airport

travel to the résumé of things the teams learned. The trainers told everyone in advance that going through security would be extremely complicated, and there was no simple way to do it. The recommended method was to walk up to the security check, put your stuff on the conveyer belt, tell your dog to sit, and then have the security person take your hand and help you through the checkpoint. Then, when you reach the other side, call your dog forward and have the animal hand checked.

"It takes a lot of patience," Smitty told Brenden. "These people are just not educated about how to handle working dogs. You're going to find that in the real world you and your animal will face a lot of experiences where you'll say to yourself, 'How can people be so dumb and insensitive when it comes to understanding that you and your dog are a professional team and need to be allowed to do your job correctly?'"

Brenden actually had a comical experience the day they were in the airport. He sat at a gate with the big dog at his feet, waiting for the rest of the class to complete the exercise of getting through security. A mother with her little boy approached him and asked if her son could pat the handsome black Lab. Brenden made the mistake of saying it would be fine. But then he was amazed when he heard the kid scream as Nelson decided to share the little boy's ice-cream cone. The child was upset, the mother was upset, Nelson was upset, and Brenden, well, Brenden couldn't help but find the whole incident pretty funny. It did remind him, however, that letting people pat Nelson when he was working was simply not a good idea.

On the night before he and Nelson were to leave the guide

school and go out into the world, Brenden couldn't sleep. At some point in his tossing and turning he got out of bed, put on his bathrobe and slippers, and sat at his desk, drumming his hands in thought. *Could life really hold meaning for me? Will the independence I have gained really work? Is the success Nelson and I have achieved just a mirage, something artificial that the world will shatter when we get home? Will Lindsey ever see me as a whole person, or will she break my heart? And if that happens, then what?* All of these thoughts sent him back into the dark despair that was always at the edge of his consciousness. Brenden tried to put those thoughts out of his mind, reaching down to pat the big dog, who was also awake and had moved over from his place at the side of the bed to lie with his head resting on the man's foot.

The newly minted master caressed the big animal's soft ears. *Velvet*, he thought. *They feel like velvet in such contrast to the coarseness of the fur*. And yet in the contrast of the touch, the dual nature of the animal was revealed, from hard work and discipline to the ultimate in softness, kindness, and love.

Brenden dropped to the floor, running his face along the dog's neck, taking in his smell. It was a dog's smell, but Brenden had come to love it, and he could separate the smell of Nelson from all the other animals in the school. Nelson's smell was—well, Nelson, and Brenden appreciated it beyond all comprehension as he took in a big whiff.

The dog breathed softly and slowly, completely contented as the man's hands roamed over him. Brenden had already learned to read his friend's breathing. He knew when Nelson had to relieve himself. He understood immediately when the animal felt tension, as the guide dog's breathing would become shallow and quick. He loved it when Nelson would quiver with excitement and enthusiasm, vibrating from the tip of his nose to the bottom of his paws. *And those paws: slightly webbed and just as good for swimming or running.* He kissed the dog's nose and got a lick in return.

"We're going to make it together, boy," he said to the dog. "You're going to help me make it."

As he climbed back into bed, the animal's tail said yes in response.

Graduation day dawned clear and bright with promise. Everyone dressed for the occasion, most especially Jimmy, who decided to attend the ceremonies in full tails and high hat that he rented from a store downtown.

"Why the formal duds?" Smitty asked Jimmy, laughing.

"Because I'm too old to ever get married again," the man said, patting his golden retriever, "and this beautiful girl is going to be my most important partner for the rest of my life, so I figured a fella should dress for the occasion."

Smitty wasn't laughing anymore, and his hug told Jimmy he understood.

Brenden found himself particularly moved by some of the comments from the speech given by the president of the guide dog school.

"Graduates," he told them, "it's our great hope that the eyes of your guide dog will open worlds of possibility to each and every one of you. In your time with us, I know you've come to love your animals, and you've begun to understand that the interdependence that you share with these remarkable dogs will create the independence we know all of you very much want.

"Your dogs are not only your working partners; they will also serve you as loving companions. I think you've probably figured out that with them you can enjoy almost limitless activity, and there's no reason why you can't pursue any career goals you have in mind. I think you'll also find that people in general will very much want to get to know you because you have a beautiful working animal as your best friend.

"You have a lot to look forward to, and as the trainers say, 'You haven't even touched the tip of the iceberg when it comes to the potential that you and your dog will share as a working team.' The trainers call it seasoning, and when graduates come back to see us, they often talk about how much the work changes over time. One of these folks recently told me that he can't remember the last time he gave his dog a formal command. He said they have conversations, and sometimes he feels that the animal is talking back."

Everybody laughed, but each student and trainer knew exactly what the speaker meant.

Guide work creates a connection between man and dog unlike any other in the world. The intimacy can only be compared to a marriage that stands the true test of time and grows in love and communication.

Brenden reached down and stroked the head of his special new friend lying on the floor next to him.

"Nelson," he said quietly, "when I came here, I didn't know if I really wanted you, and I certainly didn't believe that I'd learn to love you."

The big dog's tail thumped the floor, and Brenden smiled as he removed his hand to stop the wagging.

When the graduates were called up individually with their dogs to accept their diplomas, Brenden was surprised to find tears in his eyes. This time, however, he understood that they were tears of joy and relief that he had succeeded in surviving the month-long program at the school. Now he would be taking his dog and going into the field, hoping to begin a new life.

He was further touched by Harold Smith's emotion as he said good-bye to the old trainer. He sensed that along with his own tears there might be just a few in Smitty's eyes as he hugged Nelson, no longer trying to hide his feelings for the big black dog.

"He's the best I've ever trained, Brenden. If you use him well, you both will get better and better at the job, and you'll find the freedom I know you're looking for."

"I wish I was as sure as you are, Smitty," Brenden said, giving the trainer a hug. "I wish I was as confident as you are."

The man reached into his pocket and handed Brenden a pair of socks.

"What's this for?" he asked, surprised.

"We always replace items that our dogs destroy," he said, smiling. "But you know what, kid? You'll never have to worry about anything like that anymore. I can feel from his eyes that Nelson has made a decision that you're his master and he loves you. Now, what is it that I always tell you?"

The two men intoned it together. "Trust your dog."

chapter sixteen

The flight home from California was uneventful, except for a little eighty-five-pound thing called a black Lab so nervous that he had to climb up on Brenden's lap as they took off. Eventually, the big guy settled down on the floor under the man's feet, and by the time they landed he was an old pro, not even stirring as the 767 touched down in Denver. Brenden told his mother that he and Charlie would drop her at home; he planned to visit Lindsey as soon as they arrived.

As the plane droned on, Brenden said a silent prayer. He had to admit that he was more than just a little uneasy about his coming reunion with Lindsey. Over the last month, he had often asked God for guidance as it related both to his disability and to his relationship with the girl. He felt like a tightrope walker—a man on a high wire—in balance but always on the edge of falling, secure but not safe in his teetering sense of self-worth.

Lindsey loved him. He had to believe that. But he also realized that the stereotypes surrounding disability must affect the way she perceived him. To her, Brenden was handicapped, and Lindsey was about perfection. Over the past week, he had heard too many excuses about her busy schedule not to realize that Lindsey put Lindsey first.

Although Brenden had grown in empathy and compassion while learning to deal with his blindness, he had no idea how self-centered his own attitude was toward her. It didn't occur to him to consider what beautiful Lindsey might be taking on in committing her life to a blind man. It never crossed his mind that perhaps in the interest of her happiness, he might at least offer her a choice in the matter. He only wanted to confirm that she loved him enough to accept his blindness, and he needed to find out now.

After dropping Brenden's mother at home, Charlie drove him downtown to Lindsey's Larimer Square apartment.

"Listen, Charlie," Brenden said, "I want you to leave Nelson and me a block away from Lindsey's door. It's important that we arrive at her apartment on our own. It's part of what she has to see."

"I get it, pal," Charlie said. "Do you want me to wait?"

"Not unless you intend to stay outside all night."

The other man laughed, slapping Brenden on the shoulder. "Okay, dude, forget it. Good luck."

During the walk to Lindsey's apartment, Brenden took slow, deep breaths, trying to settle his nerves, trying to put himself in a place where he would exude confidence, a place where Lindsey would feel that she was seeing the old Brenden—a guy with a can-do attitude, a person imbued with enthusiasm, someone who could handle anything. Most particularly, he wanted her to see a man who could love her and whom she could love unconditionally.

LINDSEY KNEW THAT BRENDEN WAS coming home today. She figured that meant she'd have until tomorrow before she had to face him. Surely he would spend the day with his mother, getting settled in again at home.

Last night she had gone to a party where she drank way too much, and now she was not only hungover, but some guy named Danny or Eddy was in bed with her. He was a little man with little manhood in comparison to Brenden, but there he was, and she had slept with him, because she needed to hate herself enough to end her relationship with Brenden.

In some odd, backhanded way, she could better handle blaming herself for failing morally than for being unwilling to face his blindness. *I'd rather be a loose woman than a cruel and selfish one.* At least that's what she thought as she lay there in bed beside what's-his-name.

Her doorbell rang.

She glanced at the clock. Four in the afternoon, and they were still in bed. She was wearing only a T-shirt.

"Who the heck is that?" the guy asked, as if he had any right to be there.

"I don't know," Lindsey said. "Let me find out."

Crossing the living room, she pushed the intercom. "Yes?" she said, still groggy and half-asleep.

"Hey," Brenden said, his voice full of enthusiasm, "that doesn't sound like my Lindsey. That sounds like a girl who has been studying too much or is hungover."

Lindsey started to shake. "Oh no, Brenden, oh my—"

"That's right, baby," the voice said through the intercom. "It's your Brenden with a new friend for you to meet. Open up, sesame."

Brenden heard muffled voices through the intercom.

"Lindsey?" he said. "Lindsey?"

"Just a minute, Brenden."

More muffled voices, and his heart went cold.

Now he could hear water running and the sounds of—what was it—another set of feet on the floor? Wow, he was getting too good at this blind stuff. He was getting to where he could hear everything.

Thirty seconds later the buzzer signaled that he could open the door. The man and the dog climbed up the one flight to the girl's apartment, where she met him on the landing, trying to put up a good front. Her arms went around him, and she attempted to kiss him, but there was a smell—of what? Of nighttime. Of lovemaking. Of someone else. Brenden knew it in an instant, and he felt the big dog tense in the harness, suggesting he saw something or someone through the still-open door.

He pulled away from the girl's embrace, appealing to her with his blind eyes. Brenden's voce was incredulous. "Lindsey, what is this? I love you."

The young woman was desperate, understanding that Brenden knew she wasn't alone. "I love you, Brenden. I love you very much." Her voice rose. "No. Please. This doesn't mean anything. He doesn't mean anything."

Being caught out, Danny or Eddy, or whoever he was, slunk back into the apartment, trying to find his clothes, and Brenden heard everything.

"Couldn't you have waited, Lindsey?" he said. "Couldn't you at least have waited until I put some of the pieces of my life together? Did you have to shatter my life and then step on the broken glass?"

"Brenden, wait," the girl entreated. "Please wait. Let's talk about this. I just wasn't ready to—"

Brenden cut her off. "To what? To deal with a blind man? Someone whose eyes can't see how beautiful you are, Lindsey? Well, maybe that's just as well. You may look great on the outside, but on the inside . . . on the inside, Lindsey, you're ugly as a corpse in a cesspool."

The girl tried to hold him again, but he pushed her violently away with his free hand as he gave the dog the command. "Nelson, downstairs. Find the stairs."

The dog did exactly what he had been trained to do, turning 180 degrees and placing his master's feet squarely on the edge of the staircase.

He heard her sniveling and could tell she was in tears, but he didn't wait. "Forward, Nelson," he said. "Outside."

Brenden didn't even reach for the banister as the team descended the stairs with elegance and confidence. Lindsey watched them, amazed in spite of her distress.

On reaching the street, Brenden became an automaton. He was lost in his pain, unable to connect to his present, unable to gain support from his past, unable to consider something as simple as an immediate future that would take him—where? Home? Some bar? Another woman? He didn't know, and he didn't care.

Life, fate, God had dealt him another blow. He had prayed for help, prayed for a small miracle, prayed for love. And now, now there was nothing, only the emptiness that arises from a broken heart and a shattered spirit.

Over the next few hours, Nelson became educated on another side of life as Brenden found three bars along the way. Irish whisky with a beer chaser. He didn't know how many he drank. He only knew that by the time darkness settled over Denver, he and the dog were still walking, and the animal still performed perfectly. Walk a straight line, come to a curb, cross a street. Walk a straight line, come to a curb, cross a street. Don't bother to listen for the traffic. The animal would take care of him. That's what Smitty said.

As for Nelson, he found that it was more difficult to keep his master going in a straight line. Brenden was tired, very tired. Tired of everything. Tired of struggling. Tired of fighting for a life that now had no meaning. Tired of feeling less than a whole person. So tired of being blind.

Why not take a rest? Why not just find a quiet place to sit down and rest? Why not do it in the middle of the street? See what would happen. Just sit in the middle of the street and see what would happen.

The dog moved him forward to another curb, and for the first time Brenden listened for traffic. None. *It must be a side street,* he thought, *someplace off the beaten path where a man could just sit or lie down and rest.*

"Forward, Nelson," he told the big dog.

They stepped out into the street, but halfway across, Brenden dropped the leash and let himself sink to the pavement.

For a moment, the dog stood next to him, confused. What was going on? Why was his master sitting down? This wasn't right. He had to get Master out of the street. The dog raced to the other side, jumping up on the curb and turning to face Brenden, his eyes imploring his young friend. *Come on, come on*, he tried to say. *Come with me. Get out of the street.*

The man dropped his chin to his chest and sat motionless. The dog raced back to the middle of the street, grabbing the man's jacket and pulling hard, trying to drag Brenden to safety.

The man lashed out with his free hand, striking the dog hard on the side of the shoulder and causing the animal to yelp with pain. Jumping back, the dog tried again, pulling even harder on the man's jacket, ripping the sleeve. This time the blow caught the animal squarely on the jaw, hard enough to loosen a couple of teeth.

Now adrenaline drove danger signals through the big dog's body, and when he grabbed Brenden's arm, he locked his teeth deep into his master's flesh, pulling with all his strength.

Brenden cried out as blood spurted from the wound. "No, Nelson. No!" Flailing out with his free hand, he missed the dog's face by mere inches. "No. Leave me alone. Go away."

The man's cry of pain caused the dog to release his hold and stand, panting over his broken master. *What to do?* Every instinct told Nelson that this was wrong. His training said it, and his capacity for survival said it, but he could not leave his master, and so he did the only thing left. He lay down next to Brenden, placing his head on the man's knee.

Out of some fundamental need for love and intimacy, Brenden reached out to pat his friend's head, and the dog responded, licking the man's hand, then trying to lick away the blood from the wound.

Brenden was crying now. Somewhere in the back of his mind another picture formed. There would be a car coming down the street any second, and he would be dead. Fine. But so would Nelson.

No. That can't happen, he thought. *Something this good can't die. Something with this much love to give can't end.*

"Nelson," he said, his voice croaking out the name. "I love you, Nelson." And with that statement, the man knew he had to stand up, get out of the street, get to safety, find his way home, try again.

If an animal could love you enough to lay down his own life for your survival, then you had to love yourself enough to keep on living.

Brenden leaned on Nelson and pushed himself off the ground. The dog was immediately at heel, his eyes looking up at his master, pleading for the man to pick up his harness and get out of the street.

In seconds they walked to safety, and in a few minutes they found a friendly passerby who called them a cab and sent Brenden home to a shaky but new beginning.

chapter seventeen

The introductory meeting between Nelson and Gus was a psychological study in contrasts. Initially, Nelson's view of the aggressive West Highland terrier was that nothing that small should be making so much noise and asserting so much aggression. Gus ran around the big dog, growling and barking, making it clear that this was his house, his territory, his family. Brenden managed to take off Nelson's harness and leash, then stumbled off to bed, leaving the animals to get acquainted on their own. Without Brenden to back him up, Gus gave one of those *feet, don't fail me now* reactions as he backed off while still trying to posture his ownership of the house and everyone within it.

DURING THE FIRST THREE DAYS, the new acquaintances argued over the possession of toys, food, and space on Brenden's bed.

Things began to smooth out when Gus realized that Nelson clearly knew his place in the pack as the new dog and understood perfectly that Gus had to be the leader. Once this was established, an amazing friendship quickly developed. In fact, ten days or so after Brenden came home, the two animals stopped trying to sleep on his bed but lay next to each other head-to-head on the soft doggy bed Mora brought home for them to share. They even learned to eat side by side without trying to take the other's food, and when Gus sat in Brenden's father's chair during dinner, Nelson was content to lie at its base. Both of them seemed to feel an integral part of the family unit, giving the impression that they were sharing in the evening's conversation.

Mora did not press Brenden for details of his homecoming with Lindsey. She was surprised when a taxi arrived late that evening and her son staggered in, steadied by the black dog's careful guiding.

Brenden had slept the deep sleep of a young man who needed it, and when he came downstairs late the next morning, Mora felt that she simply should not ask him any questions. Nor did Brenden offer any information, but she noticed that he was remarkably quiet and turned inward.

For his part, Brenden understood that the big dog had saved him from himself: a debt he could never repay. He found that he was taking stock of himself, as it were, adding up the inventory of his life—what it was all truly worth.

Mora watched him playing with the dogs in the yard and listened to his conversations with Charlie. She believed that her son had turned the corner and was beginning to develop the mechanisms necessary to cope with blindness and with life. She also was pleased to see that he had once again resumed physical fitness. He spent hours in the garage lifting weights and riding a stationary bike, working to regain his muscle tone and physical well-being. She was even more pleased when after his first week at home he told her that he would return to the rehab program in order to enhance his computer skills.

"They've got a lot of stuff for the blind, Mom," he said, using the word *blind* in an easy manner. "There's voice actuation for almost everything. I don't really think I'll have to learn Braille, except maybe to write out labels for my clothes or food or anything else I might need to identify when I move into my own apartment."

Now, that sounds great, Mora thought. *He's already thinking about the transition to independence.*

"Thank you, God," she said, remembering to offer up a prayer. "Thanks for helping Brenden begin to see the road back."

LINDSEY MADE CALL AFTER CALL, trying to get Brenden to talk to her. The messages she left became more and more imploring and emotional, but Brenden responded to none of them. She wondered if she should simply show up at his house and demand to see him, break down the door if she had to. But something stopped her. What was it? Was it possible that he had no interest in continuing their relationship? Deep down inside she didn't believe that could be true. She was Lindsey

Reynolds—smart, sexy, beautiful Lindsey Reynolds. She could make a young man do anything if she wanted it enough.

What she had to face after ten days of crying and agonizing was that she really only wanted Brenden to forgive her. She couldn't stand the guilt, and a word of forgiveness would shut down the relentless voice of her conscience. But she finally shut up that voice by acknowledging that it was all for the best. In truth, she realized that she didn't want to marry anyone with a disability. That was the reality that finally stopped her from attempting any more personal contact with Brenden.

BRENDEN ALSO THOUGHT ABOUT THEIR relationship and came to his own surprising conclusions. Lindsey had been a trophy, he decided. A trophy that really mattered when he could watch other men envy him. Their relationship had been, for the most part, physical and vapid. They had not really shared intimacy, not in the adult way he had seen intimacy shared between his father and mother, not in the way he had heard it expressed when Counselor Barnes discussed his marriage. Lindsey and Brenden probably wouldn't have made it anyway, even if fate had not taken his sight.

In the end, there's always a plan for our lives, he thought. *The secret was to have faith and read the signs God placed in one's way. Had Barnes been right? Could every disadvantage be turned into an advantage if you were willing to investigate all of the possibilities?*

"Well," he decided, patting Nelson's head on a beautiful

Colorado morning after a big breakfast his mother made for him, "I suppose it's time to find out."

Brenden could tell that counselor Marvin Barnes was delighted to get his phone call. He held the phone at least two feet from his ear to avoid going Helen Keller when the big man's voice came booming down the line.

"Well, young Brenden McCarthy. So you've been to the guide dog school and brought home a pooch? Good for you. Good for you. I've thought about having one of those myself, but my wife loves cats. We have two of them, Persians, you know, very communicative animals. And with this knee, even though I can ski pretty well, I don't do that much walking, so I figured a dog might be a waste. But I'm looking forward to meeting your Nelson. When are you coming in to visit me?" Barnes went on without giving Brenden a chance to avoid the appointment. "Tomorrow at two o'clock. That'll be great, right, kid? You remember where it is—the office at the end of the hall."

Before Brenden could say anything, Barnes hung up. Brenden chuckled to himself as he replaced the receiver. "I guess he thought I might get cold feet and look for a chance to get out of seeing him. He could have been a great insurance salesman. He's a heck of a closer."

The next day Brenden took a cab to Barnes's office and also got directions to take the light rail home after the meeting.

"I'll call you when I get close to the house, Mom," he said, walking out the front door with Nelson guiding him purposely. "I'll call you after my meeting, and you can meet me at the train."

Mora couldn't help it. Her throat tightened as she watched her handsome son step through the door and begin to navigate his way back into the real world. She continued to watch as the young man and the dog moved down the front walk and found the door of the taxi.

"For the first time I'm feeling hope," she told herself, "real hope."

WHEN BAD NEWS BARNES GREETED Brenden with a crushing handshake and a bear hug, Nelson grew protective and pushed himself between the two men, not growling, but warning the ex-Denver Bronco that the dog was responsible for his master.

Barnes registered the information and chuckled. "Looks like you're never going to have to worry about a fight in a bar as long as you have that big fella with you," he said. "I know he's new, but it seems that the two of you are already pretty tight."

"My trainer said that would happen," Brenden explained. "The work does it. I mean, the dog has a purpose and you have a purpose. You kind of need each other."

Barnes banged his hand down on the desk. "Isn't that what I told you, kid? I told you that there was independence, dependence, and interdependence, and that life would start to take shape when you understood that idea. I don't know of a better example than what goes on between blind people and their dogs."

Brenden was surprised at what came next, surprised that he

expressed such a deeply personal thought. "So, this interdependence you talk about, is that how real love is expressed between people?"

Barnes sat back in his chair. "You got that right, Brenden," he said. "Interdependence carries with it the concept of sacrifice: one person giving to the other without reservation or hesitation and doing it out of love. People can seem to be in love, giving all the right impressions, but still be selfish. To love selflessly is a constant, quiet kind of thing. It's our greatest gift. In the end it's what brings us the most satisfaction in life. You see it every day with Nelson. He's your best example.

"So, now that you've got this big spanking new animal to take care of you, how are you going to take care of yourself? Where do you want to live? And more importantly, how do you want to pay your rent?"

"I don't know," Brenden said. "I think I told you that I was just beginning my internship as a medical doctor and that I thought I was going to be the next world-class orthopedic surgeon. But now I just don't know."

Barnes thought about it. "Didn't you tell me that you did your premed work with an education minor? What about teaching? Biology or chemistry or something like that?"

"I don't know," Brenden said. "I don't think I'm cut out to be a teacher. I don't have that kind of patience."

"Okay," Barnes said, scratching his head. "What about research? Something in the scientific field? Did you like science enough to give that a try?"

"No! Not really," Brenden told him, laughing. "Sure, I got

through the science courses—all the chemistry and stuff—but it was really only to go to med school. I don't think I ever would want to spend my time in a lab, and anyway, I might have trouble mixing up the formulas. You know, pouring dangerous acids into test tubes."

Now Barnes laughed. "You know what, Brenden? You're well on the way to good health because at least you're beginning to develop a sense of humor."

The young man smiled. "I suppose if you can't laugh at yourself, you can't laugh at anything."

"You got that right," Barnes said. "Humor is the best medicine there is." The big man drummed his fingers on his desk. "Look, Brenden, it might be too early to suggest this, but what about using your medical degree as a practicing doctor?"

"What do you mean?"

"I mean, finishing your internship and then doing your residency in psychiatry. As a psychiatrist, you'll be working with other people who lose their sight along the way, or," he quickly put in, "anyone who has problems to deal with. It seems to me you already have the most important element in place."

"What's that?"

"Empathy," Barnes said. "I think you're one of those guys who would be very empathetic when it comes to thinking about the problems of other people."

Brenden sat back for a minute, listening to the clock as he thought about it.

"I suppose I could finish my internship and then look into the possibility of doing a psychiatric residency somewhere."

Barnes leaned forward, enthused. "That might be terrific, Brenden," he said. "I'd be happy to help you. I know everybody that's anybody in the field, at least anybody in Colorado. You could probably do your residency right here in Denver, at the CU Health Sciences Center. Their psychiatry division is excellent, and the guy who runs the department is a poker buddy of mine. Actually, he's not too happy with me because he thinks I cheat when we use Braille cards, but that's his problem. Would you like me to call him and set up an appointment?"

Brenden felt the excitement in his stomach.

"Yeah, yeah, I really would, Mr. Barnes. Please give him a call."

"On one condition, kid," Barnes said.

"What's that?"

"That you stop calling me Mr. Barnes. It's Marvin or Bad News or Mr. B, okay?"

"Okay, Mr. B," Brenden said, remembering that was what the man's secretary called him during their first meeting.

"Good," Barnes said. "Good. I'll make that call and set up your appointment. Oh, listen," he said, remembering something, "I had a little conversation with my friend, Hal O'Leary. Remember I told you about him? He's the guy that created skiing for the disabled up there in Winter Park, where I go every weekend. They say we're going to get a big dump of Colorado powder in the next couple of days. You want to take a trip up there with me? My wife will drive us. Edna doesn't ski, and she really doesn't like snow very much, but she enjoys—what do you call it? The ambiance of the whole thing. What do you say? You want to try it?"

Things are really happening fast, Brenden thought. *Maybe too fast,* but he found himself compelled to say, "Yeah, I'll go up there with you and see what happens."

The big man stood up, his chair squeaking with relief. "Okay, I've got your address. I'll pick you up Saturday morning at, let's say, 6 a.m. That'll get us up there in time for a good breakfast, and then we'll see if we can find you someone who will get you pointing downhill. Saturday morning, okay?"

"Okay," Brenden said, picking up Nelson's harness and leash. "Saturday morning."

chapter eighteen

Bad News Barnes was as good as his word, arriving promptly at six o'clock Saturday morning, along with a thermos of coffee and a bag full of Egg McMuffins.

Like so many young people, Brenden had stayed up far too late on Friday night, and the big man's early morning enthusiasm completely overwhelmed him.

Barnes loved Motown music, along with Jimi Hendrix and Janice Joplin, artists who had been current during his Vietnam experience. He not only played them at a volume that filled the SUV with a cacophony of sound, but he also sang along with most of the tunes in a pitchless voice that made Brenden question his ethnic roots.

Barnes laughed uproariously. "You're probably right, young Brenden McCarthy. I may be one of the few African-Americans I know with neither rhythm nor vocal acuity, but, buddy, I love to sing, and somehow Edna has put up with it for all these years. Haven't you, honey?"

"Mm-hm . . . mm-hm," said the big man's wife.

Barnes laughed again. "See, Brenden? Tolerance. That's what makes a good marriage. Tolerance. Now let me tell you about Hal O'Leary and the Winter Park program.

"Hal O'Leary was a hot-shot ski instructor in the early seventies, a lot more interested in the nightlife than he was in the lessons he gave during the day. He came to Colorado from Canada, where his folks were pretty well-off, so he was probably a little spoiled. It's funny how we find our way. Like I told you, for me there was Vietnam and football. You'd never think that someone with a background like that would do what I do now. But here it is. That's what's wonderful about your life, Brenden. You just don't know where the fates will take you. It's a matter of being open to the possibilities.

"Anyway, O'Leary hotdogged his way around the mountain, and the guy who ran the ski school had just about had enough of Hal's act, so he assigned him to a rather challenging situation. There was a nurse named Rhetta Steadman who worked at St. Joseph Hospital in Denver. She and I came from the same theater of war. She had been a combat nurse in 'Nam right about the same time I was there. She came home and started to work in the rehab program at St. Joe's, with both veterans and children who were dealing with disabilities.

"One day some kids approached her and told her they had always wanted to ski. At that point disabled people had never been on the mountains anywhere in the world, but this Rhetta

Steadman was really something. She called the ski school in Winter Park, and, well, the rest is history.

"So anyway, the first group was assigned to—guess who—Hal O'Leary. I love his story about that first day when a bus pulled up in the parking lot where he waited. He heard the sound of a bunch of kids singing 'A Hundred Bottles of Beer on the Wall' as raucous as it gets. The door of the bus opened and out stepped Miss Rhetta, followed by a kid crawling down the stairs. Imagine that. Hal found out later that the kid suffered from spina bifida and couldn't walk. Then along came three kids holding on to one of Rhetta's assistants because they were blind. The bus driver unloaded wheelchairs because there were also a few children who were paraplegic. And just to make it a little more interesting, Hal soon learned that some of the other kids were mentally challenged. O'Leary just stood there in the snow, flabbergasted."

"Wow," Brenden said. "What did he do?"

Barnes waited to answer while he finished chewing his fourth Egg McMuffin.

"Somehow he got them up on the mountain the first day, trying to make it work with regular equipment. The kids were falling all over the place, and no one actually skied. But something happened to Hal O'Leary; these children touched his heart. He began to think of ways to open the sport and allow them to enjoy the freedom of a downhill run. For the amputees, he worked on what became the monoski. This is a ski with two small side attachments, sort of like miniskis that allow for stability—you've probably seen them. For other disabilities, he created the ski bra—a bungee cord drilled through the tips of the skis that keeps them together. He figured out that blind people could ski the mountain with a guide calling turns. That's what you and I are going to do. And for the mentally challenged, he knew you had to have just the right kind of instructor.

"That was about thirty-five years ago. Since then, the National Sports Center for the Disabled—that's what the program's called—has taught over a hundred and fifty thousand special-needs people ways to enjoy this terrific sport. They've dealt with over a hundred and forty different disabilities in the program. No challenge seems to be impossible for Hal and his staff to take on. Winter Park comps some of their services, but the rest of it comes from donations. Brenden, I believe this is the single most important sports program for the disabled in the world. Talk about building self-worth and a true sense of self-confidence, Hal O'Leary's program does it in spades. Look what it has done for me."

And right on cue, Diana Ross and the Supremes began to sing, "Ain't no mountain high enough, ain't no valley low enough, ain't no river wide enough to keep me from getting to you."

The whole feeling of the moment got to Brenden. In fact, all three people in the van joined the Supremes in a heartfelt chorus.

ARRIVING AT THE MOUNTAIN, BRENDEN met Hal O'Leary, who was waiting for them.

"Brenden McCarthy," he said, putting out his hand as if he'd known him all his life, "I'm Hal O'Leary. Marvin tells me you might just be the next blind world's champ, and that gets me excited. We haven't had a world-class blind guy in our program for the last—let's see—about the last five years, so you are very welcome. Am I right? You did ski on your high school team and then did some racing in college?"

Brenden shrugged. "Yeah, but that was before I was—"

O'Leary interrupted. "Physically challenged? It's all relative, Brenden. Remember, you're not going to ever have to compete with the guys you used to race against, but that doesn't mean you can't enjoy the same kind of fun. Even if you decide you don't want to race, the sport is going to give you back the most important possible gift."

"What's that?" Brenden asked.

"Freedom," Hal said, sounding like Smitty. "By the way, didn't you just get a new guide dog? Where is he? We have kennels here."

"Oh, I didn't know that," Brenden said. "I left him at home."

"No problem," O'Leary told him. "No problem at all because this morning, you got really lucky."

"Why is that?" Barnes put in.

"Because Brenden's going to spend the day with Kat."

"Aw, man," Barnes grumbled. "I thought I was going to get to ski with Kat."

O'Leary laughed. "She's had enough of you, big fella. She's tired of dragging your butt around the mountain, so I'm taking you out myself to give you a real workout."

Just then, Brenden heard the sound of light feet coming up the stairs and a voice that pealed like a church bell.

"Bad News Barnes." She laughed. "Don't let your feelings be hurt. You'll always be my favorite."

"Now, that makes me feel better, Kat. Let me introduce you to Brenden McCarthy. Brenden, this is Kathleen 'Kat' Collins."

"Hi, Brenden."

The girl put out her hand, and as Brenden shook it, he found himself remembering Barnes's conversation about handshakes. This one said definite, strong, feminine, warm. He registered all of those feelings and then felt a twinge of guilt, remembering that his relationship with Lindsey had just ended. Lindsey.

"Are you ready for a great day?" Kat asked. "The snow is absolutely perfect, and I know it won't take long to get you comfortable. You just have to trust me."

Brenden noted that they were still holding the handshake, and he could sense that she wasn't pulling away.

"Have you got your own ski stuff?" she asked, finally dropping his hand.

"Oh, s-sure," Brenden stammered, getting his thoughts back together. "My skis are on the rack, and my boots are downstairs."

"Well then, let's suit up"—Kat laughed—"before the yahoos ski all the powder off."

Brenden took her arm and walked down the stairs, forgetting to say good-bye to Barnes. The big man laughed and called after him.

"That's how to dump a friend, pal. Just because she's a hot-looking girl."

Brenden turned his head and smiled.

"Sorry," he said over his shoulder. "I'll buy lunch."

Kathleen "Kat" Collins had grown up in the East and graduated from the University of Vermont, where she had been number one on the ski team, in both downhill and slalom. She had read about the National Sports Center for the Disabled and felt that it would be a great place to work while she decided whether to go to graduate school and get a master's in special ed. Kat was born to be a teacher, and now in her second winter as a member of Hal O'Leary's staff, she was the most requested instructor on the lesson schedule.

About five-five with great legs, rock-hard abs, and dancing blue eyes, Kat did not think of herself as beautiful, but no one who met her would ever forget her impact. She was as warm and bright as the sun at the top of Winter Park Mountain, and Brenden was immediately bathed by her light. She made him feel completely comfortable, both in the way she guided him and in the conversation that began on their first chair lift ride and stopped only when she began the first step in his ski lesson. Getting on and off the chair lift was the immediate goal, and Kat explained exactly how they would do it.

"Brenden, when I tell you that we've gotten to the Wait Here sign, it means that we're the next chair to go. You'll step out onto the ramp, and the most important thing is to make sure that your skis are parallel to mine. I'll watch for that. Then I want you to reach back with your right hand, and I'll count down—three, two, one—when the seat is coming. You'll feel it, and then just sit for the ride, okay?"

"Okay," Brenden said and performed his maiden voyage perfectly.

On the ride up Kat asked, "Did you ski this mountain before, Brenden? I mean when you could see?"

"Oh yeah," Brenden said, reliving the memory. "I was in the Eskimo program and used to take the train up here every Saturday morning. I know every inch of these runs, or at least I used to," he said, his eyes dropping.

"Oh, come on," Kat said, "you'll remember the runs right away, and that'll help us a lot because you'll have a feel for all the terrain changes. It's amazing how much people remember when they lose their sight. I actually think that having been sighted makes it much easier to be blind." She touched his arm. "Listen," she said, "I didn't mean to be so forward; it's just that I've seen how students who could see before make good use of the information they gathered when they had sight."

Brenden shrugged in his jacket. "Maybe," he said. "I can't say that I'm at that place quite yet. It's only been a few months since my accident, and well, I guess you could say I haven't yet accepted everything about being blind."

"Okay, okay," Kat said, giving Brenden her best sunshine smile. "Enough of this serious stuff. We're about to get off this chair, so let's get ready to ski, dude."

Despite himself, Brenden couldn't help but love the girl's enthusiasm.

"Okay," he said, "blind or not, let's go ski."

When they arrived at the top of the mountain, the young man was impressed with the way Kat took over.

"All right, Brenden," she said. "I know you've been a skier for a long time, and my guess is you've been a very good one."

Brenden smiled. "Anything and everything, Kat. Anything and everything. That's the way I used to ski."

The girl touched his arm gently.

"And you'll ski that way again, Brenden. I promise. You have a great background. Let's talk about how we'll move around the mountain when it's crowded or when I have to get you through narrow areas. It's called the human guide system. I'd like you to take my arm and ski as if we were one person. What I mean is that we'll turn together. All you'll have to do is remember that whichever one of us is on the uphill side of the turn initiates it. The other person just sort of lets his or her skis come around. But remember that the key is to never stem. You must never let your heels go wide so that we can avoid crossing."

"I get it," Brenden said. "That could be painful."

Kat went on. "I'm going to take you to Cramner. It's a wide-open intermediate slope, but it has some good pitch, and I think you'll love it."

What Brenden liked right away was the feeling of skiing with Kat as one. They glided over the snow as if they had been doing this all their lives, and he could tell that the girl felt it too.

Arriving at the top of Cramner she said, "You know what, Brenden? That was awesome. I ski with a lot of people, but that was awesome. We can go anywhere."

Brenden was full of confidence.

"So, how do we go down the hill, Kat, when I'm skiing by myself?"

"I'm going to ski behind you, Brenden, right in the tracks of your skis, and I'll either be calling the turns for you, or, if we're lucky, letting you have some freedom. Now, I want to caution you. When I tried to ski under a blindfold with an instructor behind me, I found it very scary because I couldn't gain the kind of confidence I needed to have in my instructor. Moving through space without my eyes at high speed was frightening."

Brenden was quiet for a moment, thinking about it.

"It is frightening, Kat," he said, "but I've been getting used to it, sort of, thanks to the help of a wonderful guide dog named Nelson. I'm kind of"—and he was surprised at his use of the word—"beginning to adjust, so I think I can do this."

Kat took in this information, smiled to herself, and went on. "Well, we're standing at the top of the run, Brenden, and we've got a clear space, so you can begin when you're ready. Point your skis down the hill, and I'll call the first turn."

As Brenden pushed off, he found himself extremely nervous and showed it by saying, "Whoa, whoa, whoa, whoa," as his speed began to pick up. Why was he afraid? He stopped, shaken.

"I'm sorry, Kat," he said. "I'm sorry. I guess I spoke too soon about confidence. I'm just a little—"

"Nervous?" she said. "I understand. But, Brenden, I promise you can trust me. Nothing will happen up here, except maybe you'll fall down, and that's not so bad."

"Okay," Brenden said, taking a deep breath, "let's try again."

This time when he pushed off and his speed increased, the memory of all his years flying down mountains began to filter back.

"Your first turn will be left, Brenden," Kat called. "Ready? And turn. Now I'm going to get you into a rhythm. And turn.

And turn. And turn. Traverse the mountain. Traverse the mountain. Stay in that direction. Come up a little bit toward me. Good. There's a little bump coming. Feel it with your knees. And turn. And turn."

Brenden let out a whoop of joy as the two young people began to float down the mountain.

Five turns later, Kat said, "Okay, Brenden, it's clear. You're on your own. Ski, Brenden. Ski!"

The powerful young man leaped forward, his speed doubling, maybe even tripling. His turns were perfect as he felt the fall line of the mountain flowing under his feet.

Now it was Kat's turn to be excited.

"That's awesome, Brenden. Awesome. I'm right here. Right on the back of your skis. Go. Go. Go."

And he did. For the first time since his accident, Brenden was truly at one with his body, even freer than when he held Nelson's harness. This was independence, he thought, and yet the girl was back there, and they were sharing it, and she—she was wonderful.

"We're near the bottom now," Kat called. "I'm coming up on your left. Put your hand out, and I'll catch it."

Brenden shifted both poles into his right hand and with his left arm extended caught Kat's arm, and they seamlessly glided toward the chair lift. Arriving in the line, Brenden couldn't help himself. He took Kat in his arms and kissed her on the cheek.

"Thank you," he said, meaning it. "Thank you so much. I feel alive again."

His throat was tight. His eyes were full. As they got on the chair for the next ride up, the girl let him pull himself together.

Eventually she said quietly, "Brenden, I want you to know something. That's the greatest moment I've had since I came to Winter Park. Watching you, being involved with you today, makes me understand why I want to be a teacher, except that I don't feel like I was teaching you. I feel like—"

"We were sharing?" Brenden said.

"Yes," Kat said. And knowing that it was extremely unprofessional, she took his hand and squeezed it.

They came down at the end of the day, exhilarated, to find Mr. and Mrs. Barnes luxuriating in front of a fire in the lodge with some kind of hot chocolate and schnapps.

"The drink of skiers," Barnes said. "European, but it works just as well on those of us of African descent. Have one. How'd ya do?"

The big man could hear Brenden smile. "Kat was awesome," he said.

The girl interrupted. "Hey, you weren't too bad yourself, pal."

Now Brenden turned his smile on her. "No," he said, "we were awesome."

AFTER DRINKS IT WAS TIME to head home.

"Will you be back again, Brenden?" Kathleen asked, her tone sounding hopeful.

"I'll be back," he said, "even if I have to walk."

On the ride home, Brenden was quiet, trying to understand

what had just happened to him. He had experienced freedom, and yet much like his work with Nelson, he had enjoyed this affirmation because of a relationship with a mountain goddess named Kathleen.

He was surprised that he felt no guilt over his lack of feelings for Lindsey. But then why should he? That was over. What he had just experienced made him know that life held promise and limitless possibilities.

chapter nineteen

For the first time in his life, the big dog was completely fulfilled: purposeful in his work, joyous in his play, and bonded with a love for his new master that had no bounds and grew with every passing day. Brenden and Nelson were on a new and exciting adventure, and the dog greeted every experience with the same thought: *What are we going to do now?*

Brenden took Counselor Barnes's advice and continued his internship at St. Joseph Hospital with the goal of becoming a clinical psychiatrist. He wasn't sure what area interested him. Maybe working with kids. Maybe with disabled people. Maybe as a therapist. But he knew that his life made him empathetic to those with problems they believed they could not overcome.

Charlie and his mother, working separately, investigated areas all around the medical center where Brenden could set up housekeeping. They decided that what was most important to the new team was to be able not only to navigate the hospital halls comfortably but also to live in a neighborhood setting that would allow them access to everything they needed to be independent.

When Brenden thought about how far he had come over the last few months, he was amazed. He had gone from considering ending his life to now beginning to celebrate the possibilities of a future so full of promise it was simply breathtaking. And what were the important factors in bringing him to this place? First and foremost, he knew with absolute certainty, he had gotten here because of Nelson. The dog was flawless in his work, and his commitment and companionship gave Brenden the confidence to believe that anything was possible.

BRENDEN CONSTANTLY HEARD DOCTORS AND patients alike commenting on the beautiful animal, and he was delighted to notice that most of the comments came from female interns that he was learning to size up according to their voices. He found that blondes tended to speak in higher pitches than brunettes. Height was easy to determine according to the angle of the sound. He was delighted to find that he could hear a smile.

"That's right," he told his mother. "A smile has a sound."

He was amazed at how much he could determine about a girl's physical attributes. Girls with long hair tended to shake their heads often to get their flowing tresses out of their faces.

Voluptuous women, he noted, tended to sit forward or be slightly round-shouldered because as little girls they were probably embarrassed by their early development. He could identify the leggy ladies because he could hear the sound of them frequently crossing and uncrossing attractive gams. And he could pick out any girl who was an athlete just by the way she walked.

As he worked with Nelson, he came to understand that his senses were becoming wondrously alive. The potpourri of smells that he now took in on a regular basis was unlimited and actually helped him to discern how far he was from one of his favorite eateries. As for food, his taste buds were sharpening every day. If he didn't make it as a clinician, he probably would have a future as a successful chef. Now that was an interesting picture.

Had his hearing actually become more acute? He decided it had not, but he was turning up his potential to listen to everything. A new consciousness was developing in Brenden, and he liked it. He now did not live his life on just one sensory level. Oh sure, he still missed his sight, and certainly the memories of things like color and people's faces were beginning to dim. But his sensory capacity was turning on and tuning up, allowing him to use all of his newfound abilities to their utmost.

Life was exciting again, made possible by his newfound awareness and by the confidence of his best friend—a black Labrador retriever with remarkable intelligence, total commitment, and a spirit for living that touched Brenden's heart every time he put on the harness.

Brenden was once again engaged in learning, and this pursuit of knowledge and a new establishment of purpose placed him on the same track as the dog beside him every step of the way.

"We're both growing up," he told the animal, scratching him in his favorite spot just behind the ears. "We're pretty lucky to have found each other, boy."

The dog must have agreed, because he raised his head and placed it on the man's knee.

There was a bus stop outside Brenden's apartment, and it was easy for him to take the bus north to Cherry Creek Mall for any major shopping he had to do, or to his mother's house for a home-cooked meal, something every starving student needed once in a while just to keep body and soul together.

Nelson loved those journeys because he got to play with Gus, now his best canine friend. Brenden and Mora could tell how much the two animals missed each other because whenever they got together it was party time. They would often lie head-to-head, their noses touching.

WHEN HE WASN'T ON ROTATION in the hospital, Brenden could be found on the corner of Evans and University at a great bar called Pete's University Café. This required Nelson to make a rather difficult angle—crossing busy University to the far corner—but once the dog understood that Pete's was where his master wanted to go, the rest was easy. Nelson was in his glory, and Brenden was once again engaged in an independent life.

When Brenden looked for an apartment, the most important element, besides access to St. Joseph Hospital, was to have an area where Nelson could enjoy just being a dog. Good fortune found them an apartment right next to Observatory Park, one of Denver's most beautifully pristine areas. From their home on the corner of South Columbine and Warren, the pair walked east on Warren for two blocks, which led them right into the park. Brenden had become adept at cleaning up after his friend, and he felt a certain sense of satisfaction knowing that even in this most basic function, the team was complying with city rules and the environment. The dog loved it when his master brought a tennis ball along at quiet times and broke the rules a little, relieving the dog of his leash and harness and playing a spirited game of pitch-and-catch. Brenden figured that everyone who had a dog did it. *And anyway*, he thought, *Nelson deserves a little exercise and freedom just as I do.*

Brenden was indeed exercising his own need for freedom not just in his daily routines but also on weekend adventures, when he and Nelson took the train to Winter Park on Saturday mornings so he could ski with Kat Collins.

Each week Kat picked them up at the train and then dropped Nelson off at the kennel, where he stayed while they skied.

Brenden could always read Nelson's vibrations whenever he encountered new people. The young man found himself looking to his friend for reactions with every acquaintance they made, as it became clear that the dog's instincts about human beings were better than his own.

Dogs can always tell when people really like them, and it was more than clear to Brenden that Nelson loved Kat. He had never seen Nelson behave more ecstatically toward anyone other than him. And to his delight, the girl responded in kind. Each week they dealt fifteen minutes into the schedule so that Kat and Nelson could have an elaborate greeting and a little one-on-one time. The energetic black dog would melt under the firm but gentle hands as she scratched his chest and murmured sweet nothings into his soft ears.

Something was developing between Kat and Brenden as well. He felt it every time they were together. Their conversations flowed easily. They laughed at the same things, took an interest in everything the other did, shared the physical experience of skiing, and, as in his relationship with Nelson, bonded in the excellence of their team process.

They had not crossed the line between student and teacher. Not yet. Why was he hesitant? Brenden wasn't sure. It might be carryover from his relationship with Lindsey. Lindsey broke his heart, but with this young woman, with Kathleen Collins, he felt that such a thing would never happen. There was something so good, honest, and true about her. So why hadn't he asked her out? Put the moves on? Taken a chance? He decided it was because she might turn him down, and he wasn't ready to accept that kind of rejection. Not yet.

IT WAS TUESDAY, AND BRENDEN sat on the end stool in Pete's Bar with Nelson safely tucked in against the wall. Her distinctive perfume told him she was there before the touch on his shoulder and her nervous, "Hi, Brenden. It's—"

chapter twenty

Brenden loved the hypnotic sound of the train wheels as they clickety-clacked their way west, headed for Winter Park Mountain.

It was early on Saturday morning, and the cars were full of raucous people, laughing and excited about the day of skiing ahead. Conditions were fantastic on this first week in April. Springtime had come to the Rockies. They called it "bronzing time," when you could ski in jeans and a T-shirt with the sun beating down on your body.

The weather report suggested the possibility of a spring storm bringing another foot to the mountains, and that had everybody excited.

"May be a powder day," people were saying. "Yeah, boy, a powder day."

Nelson lay next to his master's feet, his rear under the seat, his head occasionally coming up to touch the man's knee.

Brenden was in higher spirits than at any time since his accident. That chance meeting with Lindsey the other night had lifted a load from his shoulders. He knew—he clearly understood—that he had been infatuated with her but that they had not truly been in love, not in the way people needed to love in order to build a successful relationship. They had been—and he smiled thinking about it—in lust.

So what was he feeling about Kat Collins—this mountain girl who exuded so much goodness and enthusiasm? He thought that he was now ready to explore possibilities, and instinct told him that Kathleen Collins might be feeling the same way. They had talked about previous relationships—the good, the bad, and the ugly—and they had learned that their views were very similar when it came to what each wanted in a partner.

So how would he cross the line? That was the problem. And the nervousness in the pit of his stomach told him that he really wasn't as secure as he might have thought. *What if she turns me down? What if she isn't really interested?*

Automatically, he patted the big dog at his feet to gain confidence, and the animal, sensing his friend's nervousness, licked his hand as if to say, *I got your back, Master. Don't worry about a thing*.

THAT DAY THE SKIING WAS awesome. At about two o'clock, the snow started to fall. First in soft, lazy flakes that floated down from high, dreamlike clouds, and then as the storm dropped into the valley and the clouds settled over the Continental Divide, the intensity built as the wind rose and the flakes became smaller, thicker, and faster.

Kat and Brenden had just completed a run down Mary Jane Trail on the back side of the mountain and arrived at the chair lift with the girl studying the sky.

"I think we'd better call it a day, Brenden," she said, above the wind. "This is getting pretty serious."

"Aw, come on, Kat. It's just a little snow, and anyway this is probably my last run for the year. You guys close up here next week. Let's just have one more. There'll be nobody up there, and you'll be able to let me ski on my own."

"All right, Brenden," Kat said reluctantly. "Just one more."

"Last run," the chair lift operator told them as they got on. "We're closing the lifts after this. It's getting too tough up there, so make it quick, and get off the mountain."

By the time they arrived at the top, the conditions had worsened by at least 50 percent. Brenden registered the concern in Kat's voice.

"Listen," she said, "I can't really see where we're going. I mean, I can see the sides of the trail with the tree line, but bumps and terrain changes, I can't read them in this flat light."

Having been sighted, Brenden understood exactly what the girl meant, and yet the touch of danger excited him, challenged something inside him.

"We've skied this run a lot. It's an even fall line, and if you just keep me centered, I think I can actually help ski us down."

Kat's laugh held a hint of nervousness. "Oh, you mean the blind leading the blind?"

"That's about it," Brenden replied. "Let's go for it."

Brenden's senses were heightened as they began the descent. He read every nuance of the snow as his skis glided silently through the powder. Keeping his turns uniform, he kept them moving, ghostlike through the storm. Turn and release. Turn and release. Turn and release.

Over the next fifteen or twenty minutes, there wasn't much talk between the two young people, but in their working together, in their sharing, a real sense of partnership was expressed, and they both knew it.

Brenden felt the run leveling off at the same time Kat saw the outlines of the buildings below. The two skiers skidded to a stop.

"Yeah," she cried. "You did it, Brenden. You got us down."

Kat threw her arms around the tall young man. In a magical moment, without either of them expecting it, their lips touched. And somehow, even with their goggles and hats, gloves and heavy clothes, they both felt warmed, melting into the kiss.

After picking Nelson up at the kennel, they headed for a German restaurant called Eichler's to celebrate with an end-of-the-season dinner. Yeager schnitzel with spaetzle and a delicious apple cobbler gave them just the reason they needed for a long walk under the stars.

The storm lessened, and Brenden hated the thought that he would be staying in the youth hostel run by the Winter Park disabled program. So it came as a surprise to him, and to Nelson, when Kat kept walking and arrived at the mountain cabin she shared with two roommates, who were both away for the weekend.

"Hey, Kat," Brenden said, smiling in the dark. "I thought I was the blind man. Aren't you a little lost? This isn't where I'm staying."

"I know," she said, stopping under the stars and turning to face him. "This is where I live, and I'm not ready to have this evening end."

As if it were the most natural thing in the world, the two young people kissed, not with the erotic passion that Brenden had experienced with Lindsey, but with an intimacy and softness that spoke of something much deeper.

Kat pulled back, her breath coming in gasps. Taking Breden's arm and pointing it to the sky, she said, "I wish you could see them, Brenden. I wish you could see God's light show."

"You're the star, Kat," he said softly, drawing her close. "You're all the light I need."

They went inside, lit a fire, and sat, warmed by its glow and by each other.

Brenden knew that he wanted to marry Kat. He knew it at his very core, and yet the shadow of his blindness and what it meant seemed to sit between them in the firelight. Could he make a living? Could he take care of Kat and potentially a family? Would he be a burden, requiring her to do so much more than other wives, reducing him in her eyes as a husband, a lover, and a man?

SHE WATCHED THE EXPRESSIONS PLAY over his face in the light. She knew how much she loved him and how much she wanted him to be hers forever. All evening she had sensed that this moment might be the right one. She felt instinctively that he wanted to ask her to marry him. And now, as she watched his face, she saw—what? Indecision? Conflict? Fear? That was it. It had to be fear—his fear—that being newly blind he would not be able to fulfill what she needed. And so she reached out and touched his face with her fingertips, tracing the worry lines she saw furrowing around his mouth.

"What's wrong?" she asked quietly. "What's going on inside that big brain?"

Brenden reached up, took her hand, and pressed it to his cheek. "Kat, I . . . I . . ."

"Brenden McCarthy"—she laughed quietly—"are you trying to ask me to marry you?"

His sigh was audible. "Yes. Yes, I am, but maybe . . ."

She interrupted. "Maybe you won't be able to drive? No problem. Maybe I'll have to tell you what's going on in a movie when we snuggle in the dark? That sounds pretty great, doesn't it? And about your clothes, I'll have to keep them organized so you don't go out looking like Stevie Wonder. And then there will be our bills and the mail and the Sunday paper. I guess you'll just have to put up with me reading those things to you, which means we'll have to spend a lot of time together. Isn't that too bad?"

"Kat, I need to . . ."

"Brenden," she said, leaning forward and kissing him, "don't you know how much I love who you are? Who you are as a person? I love the way when you talk to me nothing else seems to exist in your world. You're always right there with me all the time. I love to look at your smile because it's so real. It comes from deep inside you. It's as if your soul is speaking to me. I love how you touch me in a way that's intimate and reserved only for us. I know you'll work hard and that together we'll have a great life because we fit and because God made us for each other."

Brenden was crying now. He couldn't help it. But he pulled it together and dropped onto his knees in front of the girl.

"Kathleen Collins," he said formally, "will you marry me?"

He was surprised, very surprised, when Kat rose and stepped around him, going to the corner of the room where Nelson lay quietly.

Dropping down to the rug and taking the dog's head in her hands, she said, "Your master is asking me to marry him and make us a family. I'm saying yes, yes, yes, if that's all right with you."

The dog stretched and looked up at the young woman as if he understood the importance of her words. Holding her eyes and reaching up, he licked her cheek and thumped his tail in a rhythmic response that said, "It's okay with me, Kat."

Brenden joined them on the floor, and the group hug said life is going to be okay. No, more than just okay, much, much more.

chapter twenty-one

As Mora watched Brenden and Charlie shooting baskets in the backyard, she considered the way he had learned to cope with his blindness nothing short of a miracle. She credited most of that miracle to Nelson, the marvelous guide dog that right now worked to bite a hole in the basketball. Every time Brenden dribbled it, Nelson tried to grab it. And Gus tried to grab Nelson while Charlie kept calling fouls on everybody.

Mora loved the peals of laughter and the enthusiastic play barking of both dogs. She heard another sound that also warmed her heart: the girl in the room with her, humming as she set the table.

She really liked Katherine Collins, especially because the girl never in any way patronized her son's blindness. Actually Kat didn't cut Brenden any slack when it came to taking responsibility for the ordinary things of life. Though she was always there to help him, he cut his meat at the table, kept his clothes organized, cleaned his apartment, and held the door for Kat like any young gentleman should when they were on a date.

They set the Columbus Day weekend for their wedding, and Brenden had done the right thing, going back to Vermont and formally asking Katherine's father for her hand.

So here they all were, including Charlie, preparing a special dinner to acknowledge the anniversary of Brenden's accident. That was the only word Mora could think of—*acknowledge*. It wasn't to honor it or celebrate it, or even to remember it with sadness. It was simply to acknowledge the fact that on June twenty-first a year ago, a major event occurred that changed everyone's life, most of all Brenden's.

The ball stopped bouncing, and Charlie fired up the grill. Moments later steaks were sizzling, soon to join a feast of baked potatoes with all the fixings, a Caesar salad, and an apple pie. All Brenden's favorites, along with an expensive cabernet that Mora selected as appropriate for the occasion.

"So what should we toast to?" Kat asked, raising her glass.

"I suppose you want me to say 'to us.'" Brenden laughed. "And that is important, the most important thing. But I think tonight it's important to toast to life and how precious it truly is."

There was a pause of a heartbeat before the people at the table clinked their glasses, as if they all were taking in the message and feeling it deep within their hearts.

"*Sláinte*," Charlie said. "Isn't that the Irish toast your dad used to say?"

"*Sláinte*," Mora intoned, and the glasses clinked again.

After the dinner dishes were cleared away, they all settled down around the fire. Nelson and Gus, who had finally played themselves out, sprawled on the cool cement of the patio, not at all interested in what was going on with the humans.

For the first time Charlie broached the subject of Brenden's last climb.

"Do you miss it?" he asked. "I mean, climbing?"

Brenden took the last sip of his wine and placed the glass on the table thoughtfully.

"Sure I do, Charlie, and when you talk about climbing, I think about how much it always meant to me. But not being able to see, well, you lose an awful lot."

Mora was surprised when Kat jumped in.

"Brenden," she said, taking his hand, "when we ski, I can't get over how much you get out of sharing the sport. You use all of your other senses. I mean, you've taught me so much about how to feel and listen, smell, and even taste. You're the guy who broke down the wine tonight, talking about its bouquet and all of its nuances. I certainly hadn't thought about any of that very much. Isn't it possible that the mountains could offer you new sensory levels that you hadn't considered before? It seems to me everything else in life does."

Brenden thought about it. "So what you're telling me is that I should get right back up on the horse and ride?"

"I think that's what she means, pal," Charlie said, "and I'd be happy to climb with you. I'm sure we could figure out how to do it."

"Well, that's just the point, Charlie. If I were ever going to climb again, I'd still want to feel that I was sort of doing it on my own."

As if on cue, Nelson stood and shook himself. Brenden called him.

"Come here, Nelson. Come here, boy."

The big dog immediately came to his master, dropping his head on the man's knee.

"Are you telling me you'd like to climb a mountain, Nelson?" Brenden asked. "Because if I'm going to do it, I'd like to share it with you."

"How would that work?" Charlie asked.

"Oh, we'd climb together, Charlie," Brenden said. "I'm not about to go up there alone, but maybe I could build some kind of special harness that would allow me to follow Nelson from directly behind. That way when the track gets narrow or we need to step up over rocks, I could read him. I'll talk to Smitty about it."

THE TRAINER WAS INTRIGUED WHEN Brenden called.

"Hm," he said. "Well, I don't know much about climbing mountains, but if you want to work from directly behind Nelson and get the most possible flexibility, it seems to me that you'd want a two-handled harness. This would give you the ability to gain your balance from exactly the way the dog moved. It would also allow you to be even more sensitive to the angles when you step up or down. The harness would have to be quite a bit longer, so that when you go downhill you can still stand somewhat straight up. I mean, you wouldn't want to be reaching all the way down to Nelson's back, causing you to tip forward. Am I right?"

"I think you got it, Smitty," Brenden said. "I think that's exactly what I need."

"Let me work on it," the trainer said. "Let's see what the boys in the shop can come up with."

Two weeks later, the device arrived. Smitty made it about three times the length of a standard harness with three separate two-grip handles spread out along the shaft. This way Brenden could be as close or as far from the animal as needed, depending on the pitch and the angle of the mountain he climbed. Also, Smitty attached clip links to the harness that would allow Brenden, if necessary, to tie equipment or climbing ropes to the big dog just in case they came to a place where the man had to feel his way up a rock face and then help the animal clamber up.

"Wow," Charlie said, studying the apparatus. "This guy really thought it through when he figured out that both of you might need to help each other. Now look, Brenden, if we're really going to do this, I'm going to be right there with you."

"I know, Charlie," Brenden said, "but it's really important to me that Nelson and I handle this ourselves. I won't be stupid. If we encounter a problem we can't solve, I'll ask you for help. And I'll certainly be asking for directions. This whole thing is about interdependence, like Smitty always said. We need to be able to rely on each other. Actually, I think that's the way all of life's supposed to work."

Charlie shrugged. "Okay, pal, but you know I'm right there for you."

Brenden clapped his friend on the shoulder. "And we're right there for you too, Charlie."

They both laughed.

They decided that their first climb would be up Grays and Torreys, two fourteeners. They knew these were easy climbs, really just walks in the park for physically fit young climbers. But as Brenden found out quickly, the problem with teaching Nelson to guide over this kind of rough terrain was that the dog's instinct was not to go for it. To him, the loose rocks and angled steps were too dangerous for his master.

And so the day began with a problem. Nelson would not allow Brenden to make progress up the mountain, and no matter how much the man asked the dog to go forward, his friend said absolutely not.

"How do we get him going?" Charlie asked.

"Well," Brenden said, thinking about it, "the issue is you don't want to confuse his instinct to take care of me, get him pulling too hard and taking chances. But we have to encourage him that I want to do this. So here's what we'll try. At least for a while, Charlie, I'll follow you, holding on to your climbing rope, and I'll let Nelson be independent. Let's see what that does."

After about fifteen minutes of climbing, with the dog moving on his own, the men once again put the harness back on and encouraged the guide dog to follow Charlie. Though he was still careful, this time he got it, and Brenden was overjoyed as they snaked their way up toward the summit, never missing a step.

Charlie found it uncanny that the dog could pick out loose rock even better than the humans. The animal seemed to have a sixth sense when it came to placing his feet just so, and when Brenden followed him carefully, the blind man actually climbed over loose stone better than Charlie.

Arriving at the top, Brenden took it all in, and Charlie wished Kat were there to see his smile.

"Wow," he said to his friend. "Charlie, this is awesome. Can you hear the trout stream down below?"

Charlie listened. "Now I can"—he laughed—"because you pointed it out."

"And how about the smell of the pines? The wind is just right, and even though we're above timberline, can you smell them? And the air up here." Brenden took a deep breath. "It tastes so fresh and light. You know what, Charlie? Even the rock we're sitting on feels good, old and warm and good."

The young men were quiet, thinking their own thoughts but bonded—as they had been since boyhood—in the shared experience of the outdoors. Only the sound of the big dog's panting broke the silence, but he, too, seemed at one, relishing the beauty of this exquisite environment.

Brenden was surprised to find the climb down much harder. Even though Smitty's harness worked correctly, he often was forced to reach down when Nelson stepped off an outcropping, and there was something frightening about groping in space for the next footfall. Climbing up, he decided, had been much easier because everything was in front of you. Going down, the trust factor between man and animal had to be even greater.

And often Brenden felt, as he searched for a footfall hold, that he was placing the dog under great stress, torquing the harness as he tried to find the appropriate purchase for his feet.

"What do you think, Charlie?" he asked on one of their breaks. "Do you think all of this works? Am I putting too much pressure on Nelson?"

"It's amazing to watch him, Brenden. When he knows that you're not sure of your balance point, he drops down, almost onto his haunches, and spreads his paws out so he's as solid as the rocks up here. Talk about adapting, Nelson really has it together."

"Thanks, Charlie," Brenden said. "I just wanted to make sure."

By the time they reached the bottom, Brenden's confidence was as high as the fourteener they had just summited. He believed he could return to the Maroon Bells. He believed he could make the climb on North Maroon that had cost him his eyesight, and he believed he could do it sharing with his two friends—the man he had known since childhood and the dog who had given him back his life.

chapter twenty-two

Brenden couldn't sleep. He and Charlie drove to the Crater Lake campground to get an early start on the North Maroon climb. The blind man accepted the idea that as he worked his way up with Nelson, the overall climb would take considerably longer than when he had sight. In fact, they doubled the time allotted to complete the ascent and descent of the mountain. They figured if they left at first light, around 5:30 a.m., and assuming a ten-hour climb with an hour of rest, they could get down by four or five in the afternoon, barring any complications.

It was mid-September, so they were still operating under daylight savings time, with sunset not occurring until around seven fifteen, plenty of margin.

They also decided to carry sleeping bags, an additional layer of warm clothing, and food rations just in case they were forced to spend the night on the mountain. As experienced climbers, neither of them took anything for granted when dealing with the capricious nature of the sport.

So why was Brenden feeling so much anxiety? Why was he lying awake in the dark? The big dog lying at his side was probably wondering the same thing because he, too, was awake, as always, supporting his master at all times and through any changes in the man's emotions.

As Charlie snored on, oblivious to his friend's tossing and turning, Brenden tried to figure out what was causing his anxiety. Was it fear of failure? He didn't think so. Was it the memories of his accident? *Not really*, he thought. It all happened so fast. The painful memories were only about his post-accident trauma, not the fall itself. So why was his stomach churning, and why was he awake? He remembered his football days and how he felt the night before a big game. Was this the same thing? Not really.

His coach once told him that there were two kinds of nervousness that people could experience when preparing to take on a major life moment. You felt instructive nerves when you were very secure in what you were going to do. In these cases your nerves weren't concerned with the consequence of your effort or the possibility of failing. They were only about playing the game to the best of your ability. Brenden remembered that at those moments his emotion was always to "bring it on, let's get started" because he was secure in his ability to quarterback the team.

He knew that people felt destructive nerves when they weren't sure of their talent, or when the fear of failure became more central than the belief in achieving the goal.

As he tossed and turned, Brenden decided that the best way

to deal with his concerns was to commit to the certainty that he and Nelson were a team, and that the team was unbeatable.

Finally he fell asleep. But when five o'clock came around and Charlie touched his shoulder, he found himself immediately alert with so much adrenaline pumping through his system that he wasn't tired at all. With the temperature hovering around the freezing point, all three of the climbers were eager to get started.

This climb was quite different for Nelson because of the nature of the rock steps that wound their way to the top of the mountain. The animal quickly learned to stop when the step was high, allowing the man to touch it with his hands, drop the harness, and step up. The dog would then get a sort of running start and leap up onto solid ground. Or, on a couple of occasions when the dog and the man assessed that the leap was a little too high, Brenden would give the animal a boost from behind until he gained his balance on the top of a ledge.

This was not to say that the man helped the dog more than the animal helped him, but as Charlie watched, he was fascinated at the ease with which the two supported each other. In the eight months the man and dog had been together, it was obvious to Charlie that their bond was completely based on trust, and it was that trust that made their work such a process of sharing.

Arriving at Crater Lake, the men stopped for an energy bar and some Gatorade with both of them truly appreciating the beauty of the place.

Here they were at 9,600 feet, overlooking a deep mountain lake as clear as could be found anywhere in the world. The water was pure enough to drink, and it reminded Brenden of how fresh water really could taste as he took in large gulps. Nelson joined him in the refreshing drink, lapping until he was satisfied.

After absorbing the water, a shiver ran down Brenden's spine.

"Hey, Charlie," he asked, "do you think the temperature is still dropping? I mean, where's the sun?"

"I know, Brenden," Charlie said. "I've been watching the sky, and frankly, I don't like what I'm seeing."

"What do you mean?"

"Some pretty heavy clouds are beginning to drop over the Divide. We could get some big-time snow, pal. Did you listen to the weather last night before we came up here?"

"I didn't. I probably should have, but I was so excited I just didn't think of it."

"Well," Charlie said, taking a deep breath, "let's get going. Assuming we've got another two hours to climb, we should be able to summit before it gets too bad."

"Okay, Nelson," Brenden said, picking up the dog's harness, "let's boogie on up, boy."

The three of them began to work their way up the steep Minnehaha Trail, and here Brenden was able to outclimb Charlie because the big dog on four feet could actually almost pull him along. Brenden laughed to himself as Charlie struggled to keep up.

Reaching the last of the campgrounds at Buckskin Pass, Brenden felt the first snowflake on his nose as he pulled his stocking cap down over his ears. Now the wind had come up.

"Sirocco," Charlie said, above the howl. "The Canadian Express. We're in for it now."

Brenden considered but didn't ask the question. *Should we turn around and go down?* He was surprised at his own reaction, as a fierce need to accomplish the mission burst out from inside him.

Patting Nelson, he said, "One more push, Charlie. One more big effort and we'll be there—you and me and the four-legged guy."

Charlie registered the passion in his friend's voice and nodded, forgetting for a minute that the climber standing with him against the wind couldn't see.

After fording a creek, they began working their way up the face of the ancient glacier, trying to hurry but also being very aware of loose rock. Here Nelson shone, faultless in his step and constantly in balance as he danced his master toward the summit.

Now they were on the last couloir, a nearly vertical face that forced them to wedge themselves against the smooth wall, looking for hand and foot holds as they spidered their way to the top. Here the dog really struggled, so Charlie and Brenden took turns supporting the animal with climbing ropes, having him follow them to the top rather than lead. *The dog is so adaptable,* Brenden thought. *He just gets it; he's a real member of the team.*

They were just feet from the summit, with the snow falling at a rate of at least two inches an hour and the wind whipping it in sheets that stung any open area of the body it could reach.

Charlie's yell, "Summit!" was barely audible over the howl of the wind, but right on cue Nelson barked as if he, too, sensed the achievement.

Though it was a special morning for Brenden, they only stopped long enough to sign the mountain ledger, eat another power bar, and take in some water.

"It's bad," Charlie said, cupping his hands against the wind, next to his friend's ear. "It's really bad, Brenden. Honestly, I'm having trouble seeing."

For the second time in Brenden's recent history, a person he loved was blinded by snow, only now he wasn't sure how he could help.

"Listen, Charlie," he said, "do you think we should hunker down in a couloir and just stay here?"

"I don't think so," Charlie replied. "Looking at the sky, I'd say this could be a two-day deal. The clouds are as low as I've ever seen them and getting worse. We have to get down."

With four or five inches of snow on the ground already, it was not only slippery, but it also became very difficult for Brenden to feel where to place his feet. Now he was really dependent on Nelson, even sitting down occasionally to slide down rocks.

Bad had been an understatement. This storm was worse than bad, and both young men, along with a focused black Lab, knew it. There were moments when Brenden could feel the animal turn his head, looking up at his master as if he were trying to will the man to place his feet just right on the snow-covered rocky surface.

For the first time in his climbing life, Charlie Evans was afraid, and not just for Brenden and Nelson. Charlie was afraid for himself. As his field of vision grew less and less, he struggled to decide whether or not they should keep going. He knew from his experience on the rescue team that calling the emergency 911 signal on his cell phone would send out a beep that could be tracked. But in this storm it would be many hours before even a fast team could reach them, and that was only if the tracking system was truly accurate. So he determined that they had to push on.

The wind gusted well over sixty miles an hour, and it was becoming almost impossible to stand upright. Charlie wondered how Nelson followed him so closely. It had to be by smell. He couldn't possibly see much in this storm, and yet the dog seemed to be performing far better than the men.

Charlie worked hard to remember the route they had climbed. Though he had been on this mountain many times before, he had never faced it in conditions that not only blurred his sight but played tricks on his brain. The raging storm made it seem that up wasn't necessarily up, and down wasn't necessarily down. The driving snow confused all angles. Where was he exactly? Looking over his shoulder, he saw the silhouette of Brenden and Nelson just above him. Waving to the dog and clapping his hands, he moved forward.

Brenden felt the dog come to a stop and encouraged him above the storm. "It's all right, Nelson. It's all right, boy. Let's go, boy, come on."

The animal didn't move, and Brenden didn't question him. "It's all right, Nelson. Which way should we go, boy? You tell me."

The big dog still stayed where he was, and in seconds Brenden understood why. The scream pierced above the wind as Charlie fell.

"Charlie!" Brenden cried. "Charlie! Oh no. No, no . . ." Brenden said to the dog, "Where's Charlie, Nelson?"

Pain seared through Charlie Evans, but the reality that he was alive gave him hope. He came to rest deep in a crevasse, with his legs pinned under something. He tried to move and nearly passed out from the pain. Looking up he could just barely see the outline of Brenden's jacket and gauged the distance at about fifty or sixty feet.

"Brenden!" he screamed. "Stay where you are! Stay where you are!"

"Charlie! Charlie! Are you all right?"

"I don't know. I'm wedged under some rocks, and I'm finding it hard to breathe. I think some ribs are broken."

"Can I throw you a rope, drag you out?"

"I don't think so, man."

"What about coming down? Can Nelson and I get to you?"

Charlie studied the face of the rock above him.

"Maybe, but if you did, I don't think you could climb out. It's a sheer face, and I don't see any hand or foot holds." Charlie was wrenched by coughing. "Oh no," he said. "Something's really busted up inside, Brenden. I'm coughing up blood and stuff."

"Do you have your cell phone, Charlie?" Brenden yelled. "Can you dial in emergency?"

"I already checked, man. It's on, but I lost it in the fall. They'd have to dial us to get a signal."

Now the cough came again, and Brenden could hear the sound of gagging as blood clogged his friend's throat, choking him.

"It's got to be internal bleeding," Charlie said, his voice weakening. "I don't know, Brenden. I don't know if I can make it."

Brenden struggled to maintain emotional control. All the feelings relating to his own accident flooded his mind, as if he were watching it on a big screen, only this time in slow motion. He was instantly ravaged by guilt.

His friend Charlie was in danger, maybe dying, and it was his fault. It was his idea to come up here. His vanity. His need—to what? To overcome his blindness? To deny its power over him? He knew that it was up to him to save his friend. But how? How could he convince the dog to keep working his way down the mountain to find help? And how would he—a blind man—be able to return and find Charlie? Could he make the animal understand? Would God hear his prayer and give him the ability to communicate with the magnificent dog?

"Charlie," Brenden called through the storm. "Charlie, we'll get help. Just hang on, Charlie. Hang on."

Brenden knelt on the ground next to the animal, cradling the dog's head in his hands, trying to look into his friend's eyes, working to communicate.

"Listen, Nelson, we have to do this alone, boy. We have to get down. We have to go home."

The dog tilted his head up toward his master as if he were listening, trying to understand.

"We have to get help for Charlie, Nelson. You're going to have to do this, boy. You can do it, pal. I know you can."

Brenden wondered if the dog was reading his fear.

"Okay, Nelson, are you ready? Let's try it, boy. Let's go."

The dog took his position facing down the mountain.

"Let's go, Nelson. Forward. I'll be back, Charlie!" Brenden called over his shoulder. "I'll be back!"

He heard his friend cough again and prayed he wouldn't be too late.

chapter twenty-three

Mora and Kat sat in the living room of Mora's house sharing a glass of wine, but not sharing much conversation. Both of them looked at the storm outside, and each tried to keep the other from seeing the worry in her eyes. Though wind and sleet were pounding the windowpanes in Denver, they both understood that up there, up on the Bells, Brenden and Charlie would be experiencing whiteout blizzard conditions.

Mora had tried Charlie's cell phone five or six times over the last half hour and got no answer.

"He said he'd always have it on," Mora finally told Kat. "He said he'd call us when they summited and then again when they got down, and I haven't heard anything."

"Do you think it might be time to alert the rescue team?" Kat asked, her voice quavering.

"I don't know," Mora said. "They're both incredibly competent mountain men, and I don't want to be an alarmist, but I think we'd better have a conversation with Aspen Rescue."

"I'll call," Kathleen said. "I've met some of those guys through Charlie, and I can probably talk to someone I know. I'm not sure what they do in these conditions. I mean, climbing at night is dangerous enough, but climbing at night in a storm like this? I just don't know."

When the Aspen Rescue team leader learned that Charlie Evans was on the mountain and that he was up there with Brenden McCarthy, it didn't take long for him to pull members together. Most of them had been up there a year ago as part of the group who found Brenden. Now the blind man and his friend Charlie, someone they all respected, were out there somewhere in the storm.

The team assembled, and by nine o'clock, with Zeon lights and night glasses, climbers began to move up the slope.

BRENDEN WAS NOT ONLY BLIND, but as the storm worsened, he was completely sensory deprived. Touch was no longer relevant. With snow covering the ground, footing was impossible to feel. He was surprised that the storm absorbed all sound. It reminded him of what it had been like when he was a boy, fishing with his father off the California coast when the fog rolled in. Now he was not only blind, the absorption of every audio cue made him deaf.

With taste and smell meaning nothing, he was—what was he? He was dependent on the black dog who moved through the darkness and the snow-covered ground with instincts cultivated long before recorded time, and love crafted in the day-to-day work of a man and his animal.

Brenden found that he was getting hoarse trying to scream encouragement to the dog above the wind.

"It's okay, Nelson," he said. "Good dog. I get it, pal. Forward. Good dog. Wait. Wait. Let me get my feet set, boy." Somehow Brenden was sure that the animal understood.

There were perilous moments when he slipped and fell, but the big dog dropped to the ground in front of him, breaking his master's slide. Sometimes Nelson would whine and come to a stop because the angles or step-downs were too high. Brenden would drop down and crawl to the edge, searching for a hand- or foothold under the snow.

In every effort, in every slip, in every movement, Brenden knew that the clock ticked on Charlie's life, and the guilt he felt about his friend's predicament became almost overwhelming.

CHARLIE EVANS HOVERED BETWEEN LIGHT and dark, consciousness and unconsciousness. The thin thread of his knowledge of the mountains became a mantra. *Stay awake. Don't sleep. Stay awake. Don't lose it. Stay awake: live. Sleep: die.* Charlie understood it completely, and with every ragged breath he focused his entire being on just trying to hang on to life. Sometimes his mantra turned into a prayer. *God, help me to stay awake. Jesus, give me the strength to survive.*

Somewhere in the back of his mind, he believed he needed a

miracle, and he hoped against hope that Brenden and Nelson would be that miracle. From his position at the bottom of the crevasse, Charlie was somewhat protected from the gusting wind, and yet he registered that there seemed to be a slackening in its violence. Shading his eyes against the snow and looking up, he saw what appeared to him to be—yes—a sliver of light. The moon began to break through the clouds. Did that mean the storm was lessening?

"Please God," he prayed out loud, "let that be part of my miracle."

There were other people on the mountain just then feeling the same thing. The haste team noted the same sliver of moon that Charlie saw, and Brenden felt the snow slackening and the wind beginning to die. But where was he on the slope? He still could not feel up or down. He tried to count the cairn steps, but they were not clear in the snow. He forgot to check his watch, so time became irrelevant, except as it related to Charlie. The dog kept him safe and kept him moving. He wondered if rescue teams were also moving. He knew Charlie's cell phone could be tracked if it hadn't been destroyed in the fall, so maybe they were up here, and maybe he and Nelson could find them.

The big dog came to a stop. Brenden felt his body tense as if he were on point hunting a bird somewhere in a sunny meadow.

"What is it, Nelson?"

The dog was perfectly still, every fiber taut, alert, focused. And then Brenden heard it too—the sound of voices somewhere out there in the snow.

"Over here," he croaked, the sound little more than a whisper. "Over here," he tried again.

Thank God the dog had a voice, and his bark reverberated through the storm.

"Good boy, Nelson. Good boy," Brenden said to the animal. "Keep it up."

The dog did. In less than three minutes, Brenden was surrounded by the rescue party, and in the next few minutes, he described both what happened and approximately where Charlie was up on the glacier.

The team leader radioed Brenden's information about the glacier to support teams back in the valley. He wondered if a helicopter could get in there. He believed it was flat enough, and maybe they could pull it off.

"Listen, Brenden, can you be more specific?" he asked. "Do you know any more about where Charlie is?"

"I'm sorry," Brenden said. "I can't help you with any other information because . . ." He spat the words into the air. "Because I'm blind."

Hearing the anger in his master's voice, Nelson leaned against the man's leg and looked up as if to say, *What's the matter, Master?* And Brenden got it.

"Listen," he said, suddenly excited by the thought, "I may not know exactly where Charlie is, but Nelson does. Take us up there in the helicopter. We'll find Charlie."

Thirty minutes later four men, along with the pilot, were crowded into the narrow space of the aircraft with a guide dog lying across their feet. With the combination of moon and Zeon light reflecting off the snow below, the helicopter descended slowly, hovered, and then skidded onto the snowy surface of the flat meadow just below the glacier.

"Okay," the pilot called, "everybody out. Good luck."

"All right," the team leader said to Brenden, "you indicated that Charlie was somewhere on the far right of the glacier. Is that correct?"

"Yes," Brenden said. "Have you been able to triangulate from his cell phone?"

"No. I'm sorry," the man told him. "It must have been broken in the fall, so it's up to you and your courageous friend here."

"Okay," Brenden said. "Okay." His voice didn't hide the tension he felt.

Dropping down to the snowy surface next to the big animal's ear, he began speaking softly, taking off his gloves and stroking the beautiful head at the same time. He remembered that every time Charlie pulled up to his house in his truck he told Nelson, "Charlie's here. Charlie's here." The big dog had learned what that meant. Charlie was the guy who always played ball with him. Charlie was someone Nelson had come to love, and Brenden used that memory to channel the animal's attention.

"Charlie's here, boy. Charlie's up here somewhere. Where's Charlie?"

The animal looked around.

"Atta-boy," Brenden said. "Where's Charlie? Find Charlie, boy."

Now Brenden pointed his hand up the mountain. "He's up there, boy. He's up there," he said enthusiastically, rising to his feet. "Charlie's up there. We've got to find Charlie. Let's go get him, boy. Let's go get him."

The dog began to animate. Did he know? Was he figuring out what his master wanted? Brenden wasn't sure, but he felt that maybe he was. And then the dog began to lean forward in the harness with anticipation.

"That's right, Nelson. That's right," Brenden said. "Are you ready, boy? Okay. Let's climb. Let's find Charlie."

The dog began to move across the meadow, up over the cairn, and onto the snow-packed glacier surface.

Brenden kept talking, kept encouraging, as the rescue team followed behind them. "Where's Charlie, boy? Where's Charlie? Find Charlie, Nelson. Where's Charlie?"

Brenden wondered how his animal conducted the search. Certainly there was no scent coming from Charlie. The snow covered everything, so there were no visual cues. Charlie wasn't calling out, so the animal certainly wasn't hearing the lost climber. So what drove Nelson across the glacier, angling from right to left, gaining the right side of the mountain? It had to be instinct, Brenden thought, an instinct born of the dog's unique need to please his master.

"Find Charlie," he told Nelson again. "Atta boy. Find him, boy."

The dog came to a stop, whining.

"Where's Charlie, Nelson?" Brenden asked.

The whining continued, and the animal sniffed the air. Had he picked up something? A scent? *Maybe*, Brenden thought, *maybe*.

"Listen," he said to the team, "call Charlie's name together."

"Charlie!" the climbers chanted. "Charlie!"

The sound prompted Nelson to bark, and the cacophony of noise cut through rocks and chasms.

"Charlie!"

NO REPLY CAME, AND BRENDEN understood why. His dear friend was too weak to respond—or worse.

The dog continued to sniff the air, and soon he began to quiver with excitement. Brenden decided to go for it all. Reaching down, he unfastened Nelson's harness and took off the leash.

"Find Charlie," he said. "Find Charlie. Go get him, boy, go get him. Follow the dog, guys. Follow him."

Nelson almost ran now, laterally across the snow. He came to a stop just feet away from the edge of the chasm where Charlie had fallen. The night-lights of the men took in the scene.

"We got him. We got him," they said over the radio to the helicopter.

HOURS LATER CHARLIE LAY IN the same hospital that only a year ago had saved Brenden. They had operated on his leg, inserting pins to stabilize the broken tibia and fibula along with controlling the internal bleeding. His ribs were heavily taped, and he was substantially sedated. Then there was the question of hypothermia. Time would reveal the extent of the frostbite. But he knew that Brenden, Mora, Kathleen, and his father were standing around his bed.

"Am I alive?" he croaked, smiling through parched lips. "Or is this just a dream?"

"You're going to be okay, Charlie," his father said, blinking back his own tears. "You're going to be fine."

"We're all going to be all right, Dad," Charlie said, through the haze of the medication. "We're all going to be fine. The mountain's tough, but we're tougher." Reaching out, he touched Brenden's arm. "Give me five, pal."

Instead Brenden leaned forward and gently hugged his friend's shoulders.

"You've got it," he said quietly. "The mountain is tough, but we're tougher, and so is Nelson."

BRENDEN COULDN'T SLEEP. HIS MIND still raced with thoughts of what he and the dog had just been through, not just on the mountain but also over the last year of change, growth, and love. He knew in his gut that Nelson had become an appendage of himself, as relevant to him as his arms and legs, senses and brain. The man and the dog were one, bonded in interdependence unlike anything he could have ever imagined.

So was he better off than he had been when he was sighted? No, he couldn't say that. Certainly he wished he could see Kat or look once more on his mother's lovely face. His love of the outdoors reminded him that he would never again look at the natural beauty of things in the same way or have quite the same freedom and independence he enjoyed before he went blind. But he had learned so much about life through the application of all of his senses and the ability to be empathetic when it came to the issues facing his fellow man. He knew without question that he had become a better person and that much of the change in who he was had been brought about by the example set by the big black dog.

Nelson was a part of him, but he believed he also had fulfilled the animal in a significant way. They were a team that would spend years together getting better at the work. He understood that much of what he learned from Nelson would carry over into his relationship with Kat. *Simply put*, he thought, *Nelson has taught me how to love, and that love, that friendship, that perfect goodness expressed without hesitation or reservation in every experience will make me a better man, a better friend, a better husband, and someday*—he smiled—*a better father.*

epilogue

Winter had ended, and the big dog had shed his coat for a lighter summer one. Life was a wonderful experience for the magnificent animal. Working daily to take Brenden to classes or anywhere else the man needed to go, along with weekend hikes and climbs with Brenden and Kat. Then there was his relationship with Gus and any other friend of his master's who was willing to play ball.

As winter turned into summer, the three became four. A few grey hairs were beginning to appear around the black muzzle.

They called the boy-human Brian, and Nelson called him his. When he wasn't working, the big dog would lie wherever the baby was. Somehow, like dogs had done from the first when they became man's best friend, Nelson had adopted another person as his responsibility.

Just now, as Kat watched, little Brian was attempting to crawl toward something he probably shouldn't have been grabbing, and Nelson was right with him, eventually reaching down and gently pulling the baby back by the seat of his pants to where Kat had originally placed him. The girl laughed out loud, making the animal perk his ears.

"You're an amazing dog," she said to Nelson. "You take care of Brenden, you love me, and now you take care of Brian. Aren't we the luckiest people to have you?"

The dog agreed with a thump of his tail.

THAT NIGHT THE BED WAS kind of crowded. Brian had a slight upset tummy, so Kat had brought him in to sleep with his mother and father. The view Nelson took of the whole situation was that if three of his family members were sleeping together, it made sense for him to join them.

Feeling the bed shake as Nelson came aboard, Brenden couldn't bring himself to tell him to get down, mostly because as the little boy worked to get comfortable between his parents, he kept looking at the big dog and making cooing noises.

Brenden turned out the light, comfortable in the darkness that had become so familiar. He lovingly took in the smells of his family—the baby's head, as clean as the child's innocence; Kat's essence—musty and magical—wife, lover, mother, friend, and all his—forever; Nelson, a little pungent from free time in the backyard. But it didn't matter. In fact, it was comforting, reminding him that Nelson represented his eyes on the world.

Getting drowsy, Brenden reflected on how things had changed. *Oh sure,* he thought, *I'd love to see again, but I still have pictures in my head of so much—mountains and sunsets and . . . I wish I could see Kat and Brian—and Nelson too—but what I have now is a dimension I didn't even know was possible.*

Am I sorry I'm blind? Oh, sometimes, but I am so blessed by this family and God's grace that I think my life's about as perfect as human beings are allowed to have. Challenge to opportunity, disadvantage to advantage, negatives to positives, growing all the time. Would that growth have happened if I had been sighted? Who would I be today, I wonder?

He was aware of Kat's even breathing and knew she had fallen asleep, as had little Brian.

How right Smitty had been way back then. Brenden smiled, thinking of their phone conversation earlier in the day. *He still can't resist an "I told you so" every once in a while.*

They remained fast friends through periodic phone calls, and Smitty had even come to visit them a couple of times. Of course, Brenden had no illusions—he knew who Smitty really came to see.

Nelson stretched, taking up a little more space on the bed.

"Hey, fur ball," Brenden said quietly. "Leave a little room for us, will ya?"

As if he understood, his best friend pulled his paws in closer to his body with a heavy sigh.

Sleep came to the whole family then—the deep, untroubled sleep of those bonded in contentment, faith, and the truest love.

Acknowledgments

To Julie Cremeans and the ladies of EDA: Words don't say enough, so thank you, thank you.

To Dr. Rob Hilsenroth: My friend, my confidant, my eyes on the mountain.

To my agent, Jan Miller: I'll keep writing. You keep selling. We're an unbeatable team.

To Dr. Thomas Larkin: Thanks for all the accurate medical information.

To my daughter, Blythe: You gave me maps, love, and support. What more could a father ask?

To Ami McConnell: Your sensitivity and professionalism made editing a breeze. To an author, that's very appreciated.

To Allen Arnold and all my friends at Thomas Nelson: Thanks for continuing to believe in me and bringing my work to the public.

To Terry Barrett, director of Training Operations, Guide Dogs for the Blind: Your help was invaluable, and your love for animals and the work shone through every conversation we had.

To my friend and trainer, Harold Smith: Every time I pick up the harness, the knowledge and feel for the animals you provided flows through my hand.

To John Zell: Thanks for all of your help with mountain rescue information and for your spirit as a volunteer, saving hikers and climbers.

To every guide dog: Through their love, dedication, and hard work, freedom is possible.

author's note

I suppose all novels are different in the way they develop. Some come out of historic investigation; others are loosely written around biographies of either the writer or people the writer has known. This novel, *Together*, arose out of two wonderful relationships that forever changed my life.

The first was with my friend and writing partner, Betty White. We met when Betty and her husband, Allen Ludden, discovered me singing in a club on Cape Cod. Not only did they do everything possible to further my burgeoning show business career, but they also were responsible for making sure that I understood that the beautiful blonde girl who came in night after night to listen to me sing was a person I ought to be taking seriously. That was Patty, and thankfully, we have been married for thirty-nine years.

The second contribution to writing this book was a relationship that Betty and I shared with another golden girl—a golden retriever named Dinah. Dinah was my leader dog, and for nine years she guided me around the country and around the world; but when her eyes became clouded by cataracts and age began to slow her down, it became necessary for me to take on a new friend that would share my work and my life. His name was Nelson, and he was a strapping young black Lab. The arrival of this enthusiastic young animal caused Dinah to believe that her life had no more meaning, so she retreated to our bedroom, crawling under our bed, unwilling to share, love, or play with anyone in our family.

Simply put, Dinah had given up on life, and I was broken-hearted, not having any idea what to do; until Betty White came to dinner. She immediately understood the seriousness of my situation and asked me if I thought that maybe, just maybe, she could help by taking Dinah into her home and into her heart. Well, the magic worked. Dinah and Betty shared just over five glorious years together. This shared relationship with Dinah prompted Betty and me to write another book a few years ago called *The Leading Lady*—the story of Tom's life with Dinah and Betty's life with Dinah.

Since that time I have had the privilege of working with Nelson, the black Lab, and then another dog, Partner, a wonderful German shepherd whose life was cut much too short by the ravages of cancer. And now a second shepherd, Edison. All these animals provided me with love, joy, and blessed freedom. So it made sense that Betty and I write a fictional novel, *Together*, that we hope you have enjoyed reading.

It is impossible for me to express the unique relationship blind people have with these astounding animals. The pages of this work cannot adequately express the feelings of gratitude that I experience every time I pick up the harness of one of these remarkable animals. No relationship between man and animal is as intimate, and no love shared could ever be more fulfilling.

We hope you have come to appreciate and understand the special bond between a blind person and their best friend. Our additional hope is that in the privacy of your own lives, you will see your own pets differently, knowing that from the toy breeds to the Great Danes, from a purebred to a Heinz 57 variety, dogs have a fundamental purpose: to love us all without hesitation or reservation. It becomes our responsibility and our joy to return that same love and affection.

Tom Sullivan
March 2008